REDLINES:

Baltimore 2028

An Anthology of Speculative Fiction

Edited by Jason Harris

Redlines Publishing   Baltimore, Maryland

www.newfuturism.com

Copy Editor-   Maya Lynn Harris

Layout Editor- Sierra McCleary-Harris

Art – Dirk Joseph

Cover Art- Jason Harris

Copyright © 2012 Jason T. Harris

All stories and art © 2012 by the individual authors of the works.

All rights reserved.

ISBN: 0615685013
ISBN-13: 978-0615685014

This book may not be reproduced, in whole or in part, including artwork, in any form (beyond that copying permitted by sections 107 and 108 of the U.S. Copyright Law and except by reviewers for the public press), without written permission from the publisher and authors of the works.

Title Page, Headings and 'Screen Text' set in OCR A EXTENDED

Body text set in Sabon

Printed in the USA by Createspace, a subsidiary of Amazon.com

The stories and their characters and entities are fictional. Any likeness to actual persons, either living or dead, is strictly coincidental.

ACKNOWLEDGMENTS

To the Creator, for life, health and the impulse of creative thought; to the Ancestors who fought because they understood the price of freedom and assigned value to me even though my arrival was less than a notion- may I live up to your investment; to my wife Christina who has taught me the day to day dedication required to be an artist, and loves me in spite of and because of my incessant daydreaming; to my father and mother who dedicated their lives to community building in their own special way and strategically placed a copy of "The Autobiography of Malcolm X" in the living room bookcase so I could discover it at the right time; to my friends and family members who provide love and encouragement even when it seems I am 'in the clouds'; to my son Zen Ayi Kwei – may this be fuel for you to reach your destiny. To my Sister Maya, thank you for lighting the fire and I cannot wait to read your work. To my nieces and nephews, Bryce, Mandela, Logan and Khali...may your dreams be without boundaries. To Adam Weisen, whose website '50 Years From Now' (http://50yearsfromnow.blogspot.com/) served as the genesis for Redlines. To the late L.A. Banks for giving me a master class during a lunch break. To all the families in the community (the Mitchells, the Browns, the Kiambus; the Josephs, the Nasirs, the Cumbos, the elders and young men in the 'Infinite Eight' Rites of Passage group, and many more)...DREAM BIG; to Mestre Cobra Mansa and the International Capoeira Angola Foundation, for providing a classroom for life and a doorway to the world; to Dr. Melvin Rahming, Dr. Harold Braithwaite, Dr. Marcellus C. Barksdale, and the many teachers who cultivated my mind with care; to Baltimore, where in a span of 15 minutes I can get lost in the woods, watch a supertanker pull into port and witness daredevils popping wheelies in traffic while I munch on a vegan crabcake- a tapestry that cannot be woven anywhere else; to Toni Cade Bambara; who articulated that a writer has be more than......to the Butler family, the Harris family, The Brown family, the Carter family, Murithii and Joy Alafia, Leon and Michelle Walker, Ayisha Owens, Anasa Troutman, Leon Smith, June Archer, Nilijah Brown, Rashidi Bowe, Rob White, Babajan, Millee Spears, Ifalawo Sangoboku, Iya Nemi Ogonkwe, Eleayse Sanchois, Donna Rose, Baba Ademola, Baba Zirakote, Maurissa Stone-Bass and the Living Well Collective. Finally, to the Parkside Writer's Salon and the contributors in this book, may this be a beginning of something sustainable and positive for the community and our work as writers.

CONTENTS

INTRODUCTION:

'A Statement Regarding the Imagination of a Community'

I start with a popular quote that gets bandied about in regards to science fiction and the future in general, courtesy cyberpunk Godfather William Gibson: "The future is already here; it's just not very evenly distributed", which in my mind, goes hand in hand with an idea put forth by another writer, Afro-Futurism Matron Octavia Butler; she stated that "humanity's Achilles heel is the need for hierarchy." These statements are integral to the motivation behind REDLINES: Baltimore 2028. Science Fiction, and technology in general, has been maneuvered into falling in line with the American class structure; a structure that has been assiduously wielded to bisect and maintain have and have-not camps. Whether through the ever present vehicles of racism, sexism, xenophobia or homophobia, the need for creating an 'other' and foisting upon it the role of rival has defined this society. It is my opinion that popular Science Fiction targets the have-nots for the consumption of whatever household gadget, comic book movie or entertainment device that is marketed to 'us'. Science Fiction in this context is not a form of inspiration as much as it's an opportunity to package the future as a product. So, while this volume can be considered Science Fiction, I would like it thought of as "Speculative Realism", a literary genre not of my own conception, but concerned with the use of setting stories in the near future as a way of provoking discussion of events that are current to a community or individual.

Every city has a collective imagination that manifests in the culture of said city: what we build, where we live, what we eat, how we learn, how we punish; the list could fill a significant portion of this book. I believe that recognition of the connections between what we build, who builds it and why it's built can determine the quality of life in a city. Baltimore is one such city where this recognition is present but the city suffers because of the answers to these questions, specifically the 'why'. After almost four centuries of existing as a city with a purpose, be it a port of call, a station of industry, a capital to a fledgling union, Baltimore is at a crossroads where the path chosen by the area oligarchy is at odds with the path to which the city's residents have become acclimated.

The methodical planning that has launched redevelopment in many areas of Baltimore allows developers to casually calculate resistance in Borg-like fashion and patiently wait for the resistance to die (as the most vociferous critics of how this city is run are Elders). We of the parental generation are too busy working to raise complaint as our parents sounds the alarm while the ground on which we build our lives shifts under our feet. The lines have been drawn to recolonize Charm City as a multi-ethnic metropolis of new urbanist chic, replete with made to order communities and industry, and more often than not, we find our communities, be it African-American,

Latino, or any of the ethnic groups that have laid a foundation in this city on the margin of this shift. The familiarity and rhythm of established communities is being sacrificed to enable the march of so called progress; the light of our dreams is being blotted out by the long shadows of the corporate community.

This of course does not jibe with what consumers of popular culture have been captivated by for the past two decades; the repeated portrayals of Baltimore as a decaying metropolis, a mainstay for the media industry as a 'gritty, urban setting.' It is unsettling to live inside the 'product', experience the dissonance between what is portrayed and what actually exists beyond the narrow frame of Hollywood's lens, and live side by side with individuals who accept for truth the portrayal at the expense of participating in the tangible. The duality cripples the voice and imagination of the communities at large, rendering them vulnerable to whims of the market. Within this context, "REDLINES" was born as a response to nurture a collective response.

So what do we imagine for our community? Several years ago I contributed a story to a website called "Fifty Years From Now." The premise of the site is to pick a city and write a 1500 word story. This idea of imagining my city in the future piqued my interest, but I wanted to hear more than just my voice; I also wanted to see what ideas came up for the near future, a way of adding a sense of urgency to this idea that would make it palatable to the community at large. Therein emerged the concept of an Exigency - a state of affairs that makes urgent demands, as several of the stories, "Ile" by Kenisha Groomes-Faulk, "The Debt" by Mirlande Jean-Gilles and "Amma's Messenger" by Alexis Skinner all skillfully articulate.

We find many of our communities in this state now, schools under-funded and understaffed, infrastructure for the neighborhood (roads, waste and water lines, electrical lines) in disrepair or in peril at the slightest storm. A neighborhood that can only count on a gas station for grocery staples exists in an exigent state. A school where students and staff cannot use the water fountains because the plumbing supplying the water is tainted is in an exigent state. While the corporate community has plans such as the "Vision 2030" plan, they do not take into account the day to day issues facing our communities, and the core function of such a plan is to set forth a vision for the business sector, not the citizenry. As writers our reaction is to talk about the issues we collectively face in a creative manner. A successful artist's work can and should feed the community imagination and validate the impulse that resides dormant in many of our fellow citizens- the impulse to imagine and bring into existence a different and better state of being. We may not have to make the choices that the characters in these stories make, but the reality as rendered is such that it cannot do anything but elicit empathy and provoke thought about one's own predicament.

"Momentary Fulcrums", the second section of this volume, brings us several tales where individuals and groups make decisions in situations that change the course of theirs and other's lives. Whether it's a terrorist group, as imagined by Raven Ekundayo in "The Revival", or a young man faced with a choice in Fernando Quijano's "Dreamcatcher", or a man facing unemployment in "Change for A Five", we find situations that speak to moments we are faced with here and now- it brings to mind Frederick Douglass, who in recalling his decision to escape enslavement stated, "I prayed for twenty years but received no answer until I prayed with my legs."

In the final section, "Redlining", we find several stories of Baltimore as imagined in the near future with little deviating from the path set before us now. Redlining is about the here and now and there all at once, with the science falling to the wayside to explore the everyday lives of people. We begin with "In My Eyes", a brilliant story of friendship and family ties written by our youngest contributor, Indirah Estelle. At the center of these stories is the Red Line itself, the descendant of the infamous I-170, also known as the "Highway to Nowhere". Tonika Berkely's "Bravebird" uses the Red Line as a setting for a Father and Daughter making their way to the child's first day of school. Devlon Waddell's "The Price of Ribbon" gives us a curmudgeon's look at 2028; "Caja Caliente" and "Redlines" both explore the idea of birth, initially in Spanish (Caja), as a nod of solidarity to the Latino members of our community. Redlines speaks to the imagined and real borders that are by-products of race, ethnicity, class, and gender.

As a community, we live in this moment where we must decide what our course of action will be- will we decide to grin and bear it, run or take a stand?

Fortunately we have examples amongst us of individuals and groups who have committed themselves to finding a way- the local farm/local food movement (such as the Five Seeds Farm and Apiary, which was established in an empty lot in East Baltimore), the Velocipede Bike Project (re-purposing old bike parts and teaching the community how to build bikes), the various Yoga and Martial Arts collectives that not only train, but are active in the community; the community based independent schools in Baltimore (the Greenmount School, Nsoroma Academy and others). I also feel that Charter schools should be mentioned as well; while on a national level the charter school movement has created controversy, locally it provides families with the opportunity to send their children to a quality school to receive a solid education when schools that a child is zoned for don't have the resources to do so. City Neighbors Charter, The Green School of Baltimore, KIPP Baltimore- these are just an example of the schools that have made a positive impact in our community.

There are dozens of cultural groups that are serving as life savers and life changers here in the city through the propagation of art, and central to this struggle to control our destiny has been the literary community in Baltimore, especially the Poets, whom I feel have been responsible for keeping the spark of our collective imagination intact. It is my hope that this volume contributes to the collective effort to shape 'Baltimore', both the people and the place, in a manner that promotes the people taking ownership of our communities. While the future owns everyone's tomorrow, it can and should be shaped by all of its participants, as reciprocity is a behavior consistent with the proper ebb and flow of the universe. It is through our creative impulses, we can conjure a world that is the product of the best of our dreams, and I believe in this possibility for Baltimore, aka Tubman City, bka our home.

- JTH

Baltimore, Maryland

(The East Side),

September 18th, 2012

exigencies

AMMA'S MESSENGER

BY ALEXIS M. SKINNER

The piercing cold stabs her lungs as she takes quick sips of air. It takes a few minutes to calm the pace of her vibrating cardiovascular tissues, but Sene's feet still tingle incessantly on the invisible concrete. Crouching low, fingertips then eyes, peer through cold metal diamonds into the pitch blackness of the street. A moment passes by before she, unblinking, scales the height of the perimeter fence. There is on the other side a grandfather tree whose bottom leaves scrape against the barbed wire strands. She reaches in that direction and, clasping the top of the fence with the other hand, reaches a foot out to rest on a thick branch. It accepts her shifting weight into the Skinner tree. Moving downward, toward its trunk, Sene feels the disquiet of the sylvan. She opens her arms wide and, stretching her palms to embrace the tree, thanks its spirit for its assistance in her journey.

As he locked the general store, Talib felt a rumbling in his stomach. It had been days since his last proper meal and the days fasting did not help the feeling. He watched his boss get into her Hummer and speed off to the checkpoint. The breeze sped up, swirling black plastic bags and emaciated Styrofoam containers from the gutter sludge of the northwest city crossroads. Things were jumping tonight. Folks going on about some lightning streaking across the Heights like the horses used to at old Pimlico, now a processing and detention center. There were brothers from down at Muhammad Mosque #6A escorting some of the sisters past the old halal restaurant storefront. They would make it home, "Inshallah," before the storm came through. Some congregants loitering outside the corner liquor store sipping spiked half n' halfs said it was just another lightning storm and that there was thunder, too. Others debated that it was yet another sign of the last days. That being said, Bethel AME was packed. No more room at the inn with revival worshipers popping out of pews like the spray from a soda bottle dropped from the 44 bus.

Further up across Northern Parkway, past Sector B's, gates, Talib could just make out the figures of freshly "Shalom Shabbat'ed" men carry their heavy black coats and loosening buttons on still starched white shirts as they welcomed a piece of the cool outside air. Walking north, they were also discussing, in reserved Talmudic tones, the significance of the lights in the sky. Wives drifted reluctantly behind, keeping a wary eye on children who orbited endlessly between them. Headed down Rogers Ave, Talib's neck burned with the heat of being watched. Or maybe it was just the heat that builds right before a storm. As unnerved as he was, he tried to shake it off. Too many scans from the Gringle Megacorp's "Watcher" satellites had passed for him to still be freaked out by it. But this scan was different. "Were they going further than chip ID?" he wondered. Lost in thought, Talib didn't even notice all of the hustle and bustle from the street die down when the usually white billboard flashed blue. But he did see the sector guards' blue light post flash a stark white. Talib couldn't help but turn his attention to it while the message unfolded across the screen indicated a manhunt in progress. Someone has breached the perimeter. They were after whoever it is so a resident shakedown was imminent. But, if they just did a chip scan, Talib thought, they should know who it is already. Whoever this is doesn't have one.

Apple Baumhauer made it home just before the scan. She had moved too slowly. By racing against the clock, she was running out of time. No one knew of the work she was meant to do—and for good reason. All they had to do was line up for their monthly chip tuning. And spend more money than they had for the rations, water and supplies (that weren't worth a damn) from her store. They weren't on— thanks to their chips—so they couldn't think any better, and the "foods" she distributed kept their brains from making the connection. The only person who didn't really eat the way she needed him to was her assistant, Talib. No point in pushing him though, Apple thought. She had watched him grow up. Was almost a surrogate mother, or could have been, had she suffered the pangs of a maternal instinct. He did what she needed him to and he never gave her any trouble. Talib helped keep the peace in the store while everyone else, lost in the complexities of their daily lives, were focused on getting their petty needs met. Besides, he was chipped, too. Smirking to herself, Apple knew there was no way he could even try to escape the grid. Besides, with his parents dead and Project ReVert out of the picture, Apple's network of general stores kept every city sector in line. No one would ever rise beyond their self-centered states again.

Sene's strides were cautious as she neared Rogers. She could feel the panic as people scurried to their respective dwellings. It distorted, for a moment, her attunement to the seeker. Seeing the harsh lights on the main streets, she realized she would need to cloak herself in order to make it. Unaccustomed to beings of her nature, the human eye would not be able to tell her from a passing shadow as she ran towards Belvedere. Sene could only hope their satellite cameras worked the same way. She whipped past a drone guard with infrared ocular lenses that followed in the wake of air created as she sped down the alley way. It turned and followed for a few steps but, seeing nothing, turned in time to miss Sene's dive into a side yard. Her heart, beating faster, stretching the limits of the body she'd incarnated in, did nothing to slow itself even after her mind commanded it. So this is life? she mused, crouching low to the ground. Even as her mind was unlimited in the present, her body, she saw, would take some getting used to.

Finally, inhaling, she found control of her breath. Sene listened for the drone as it continued its work, having clearly missed the mark. Searching for her, the shadows of the trees enveloped her. Eyes ahead, she could see her objective walk clearly into view. The trees and bushes overgrown around the abandoned elementary school made the old playground seem like the secret garden it was. Trespassers were rare since even the smallest of crimes earned a permanent stay in the detention center, but Talib handled the taser Ms. Baumhauer gave him for work in his jacket pocket anyway before he made his way in. There was a rustling of leaves a few yards away. Nervously, he pointed the taser in the direction of the noise, clicking the switch, just beyond the small patch he had planted underneath the monkey bars heavy with vines. He could only hear his breath and feel the current of potential energy ripple through his arm.

"Come out or I'll—don't get smart." Talib's voice carried to the corner, near the farthest gate. He waited. Hearing nothing else, Talib relaxed some as his attention was drawn to his patch. He saw that there had been enough light to encourage the seeds he planted to finally sprout. If he remembered correctly, the coming rain would only do them good. His grandmother had given him a cookie tin with some trinkets belonging to his parents inside, including the seeds hidden in a fancy perfume vial. Even with the promise of summer ahead, thinking about his parents still put Talib in a somber mood. He shaded his eyes from the harsh street search lights as he tried to look up into the sky. He could only faintly see the outline of the moon and the Other Worlders ship beside it. "Goodnight, Mom and Dad. I know you're looking down at me from one of those stars."

As far back as he could remember, Talib's father knew no rhymes of the hey- diddle-diddle variety and, instead, spoke to him of scientific technology. His mother, meanwhile, told him they were star people who had to change first the city, and then the world. Born during the Black Gold Gush of 2010, Talib had no problem believing them both. "See, I can

be green, too." He chuckled at his pun. "What about indigo?"
Few things unnerved Talib, but he jumped back, fumbling to
get the taser on and aimed in the direction of the voice.
Somehow his father's style of logical scientific explanation
failed to find its way into his mind and his mouth worked in
its stead.

"What the hell are you and what do you want?"

A shapely brown leg escaped from shadow, joined by
another, a pair of hands, arms, breasts, and finally, a head.
Taller than him, Sene smiled but did not move. Talib was
awestruck. Just shy of eighteen, he'd never seen a live naked
woman, except in the research function of the Gringle School.
He was smitten by her perfection and the richness of her
polished ebony complexion.

I am Sene.

Talib wasn't sure if she had even moved her lips. He
maintained his bravado. "Listen, lady, I don't want nothing
from you, so don't think you're getting store credits from me.

"You need something from me."

"Naw, I don't need nothing from you, Miss. I don't get
down like that." Talib. Look. Listen. Maybe my chip's acting

up, Talib reasoned. No, this is your reality. "Get out of my head!" Talib yelled.

Apple indulged in the boob tube on occasion. It got her creative juices going. There was a documentary on about the Other Worlder disclosure during the 2012 U.S. Presidential Election—that's what won it for Palin. Schools all over the globe were scrambling to catch up with the advanced technologies had known for millennia and humans, greedy as ever, wanted it all, particularly for space exploration and weaponry. Finally, the UN and the Other Worlders treaty led to a compromise for sharing intellectual property. Humans would learn their wisdom, but only if they submitted to the installation of the chips. She snorted at the screen. "That's why those ReVerters had to go." Apple shifted uncomfortably in her seat. She needed to find the seed before it was too late. Though the halls echoed with years of neglect, the rooms Talib had restored for his use were not in complete disrepair. He had a memory of his father and mother arguing once about technology and the revolution and the OWs.

Listening to Sene, it seemed she knew all about it, too. It

wasn't until his parents died that he started noticing that they were preparing him for life without them from the beginning. Talib saw the shadows creep over her face as she told him his own story. Once his initial shock wore off, he managed to convince her to wear one of his mom's old dashikis. He would have not been able to concentrate if she had remained in her natural state. As the wind pounded the rain outside hard against the building, Talib had a fleeting thought that perhaps, Sene brought the storm on after all. Her hair, braided back against her scalp left drops of water where it brushed her shoulders. She sat there, beautiful, regal, in the way that women who knew everything could be. Inside the school, the cemented windows kept the searchlights out, but Sene, laughing at herself, radiated independently after she tried to drink a gallon of water in one gulp. She learned quickly that human throats have their limitations. Talib, sipped his slowly, still unsure if he understood what she was, even though it felt like she could see through him.

"Your mother allowed you to be chipped in the public program, because your father, working with renegade OWs, had already equipped you with a superior chip." Talib, felt suddenly lighter. He had always felt apart from his age mates, but it seemed, now, that Sene was clearing some fog.

"But how do you know?"

Sene knew this would come. She looked at Talib. His eyes searched hers for something resembling a truth he could understand.

"I am Sene Amma Titiyayne, an emissary from another dimension. I have been sent to spark the exchange."

"Exchange? Dimension?"

"Are you surprised? This world is not all that you see. Haven't you learned from those you call the Other Worlders? We are surprised it has taken this long."

"What is being exchanged, Sene?" Sene closed her eyes and put her finger to her lips.

Energy, currently.

Talib turned his head, glancing at the wall behind him that housed his book collection. Familiar titles looked back at him, many, better suited for a college library. Only military folks go there now, he thought as he faced Sene again. She was waiting for him to do something, but he had no idea what that something was. Unable to focus, Talib closed his eyes, inhaling deeply, like his mother showed him when they used to practice yoga together. He exhaled, grounding his thoughts on the cycle of breath and loosening his body. The day's surprises had manifested in tension in his chest. Lifting his shoulders up to his ears, Talib held them there until he exhaled again. Sene began to sing in a hushed tone. Though, Talib couldn't decipher the words, her low voice calmed his nervous energy.

He thought it was a chill passing through, but found himself vibrating from his feet up to his head. Keeping his eyes closed, in spite of himself, Talib found that he was beginning to understand Sene's song. And he felt his head pulsate. It reminded him of a headache; only, it was soothing—almost blissful. His eyes shot open. Sene was still singing with hers closed. Talib focused his energy in her direction.

"I chose to come here, didn't I? But I forgot what I was supposed to do."

Sene looked at him, smiling. "Yes, Amma sent me through the bummo to remind you."

"The what?" he replied.

"The bummo." Sene crossed her hands, studying them

intently at them as she attempted to form two carrots with them. She cast a bird shadow across the room, explaining,

"It's a sort of bridge between our dimensions." Trying again, "Amma dug a hole and anchored it. He planted me in it, but I had to find my way to the other side. To you."

"And this Amma person, is he a physicist?"

"He is the eldest spirit among us. I think you'd call him a god here." Skeptical, Talib seemed to distance himself from the idea. "Not the way humans understand it. He taught us how to turn thought into matter and gave his powers away, save for one. Amma's sole duty, now, is to lead the dead spirits home." Talib opened his mouth to speak, but waited for his mouth to catch up with his mind. "How long have I been here, Sene?"

"It doesn't matter. Time is action. The potential of activity is future; the summation is past and now is upon us. We must move." Talib was nervous.

"I work for one of them."

"She knows who you are, Talib. She's been expecting me. And, now that she knows I'm here, you must be on your guard."

"Apple Baumhauer?" Talib let the name resonate in his mouth. Sene watched Talib as he considered the implications.

"She doesn't know about your garden, does she?"

"No one does." He chuckled to himself shaking his head. "Just me and my folks, but they won't tell anybody." Shaking her head knowingly, Sene began,

"The star people."

"Yeh. Funny, that's what my mom always said."

"She was right. They were from the same place I am from, the star system Albararu." Sarcasm dripped from his mouth, "I should have known. Go ahead." Talib looked at Sene, waiting for further explanation. "You might know it as Sirius? We have been here for a long time, but we vibrate at a different frequency, so few on Earth have been able to interact directly with us. Your parents, like you, chose to incarnate in this dimension. They are twin spirits who worked together to raise consciousness here. And they were making great progress, too--" Talib finished Sene's sentence for her, "--until the Other Worlders had them assassinated." He sat, serious, letting the information wash over him. "They aren't from Abra—Sirius, too. Are they?"

"We have acted as planetary care takers since Earth's beginnings. The Other Worlders...," Sene broke off, "They have a different agenda."

"And you came here to help me stop them. Does that make you my twin?"

"You already know."

The rain continued into the next morning. As Apple pulled her truck into the store lot, she was puzzled. There was no line out front and Talib was not waiting for her. "Is there a resident lock down?" she wondered. Walking to the corner, she looked across Northern Parkway to Sector D. There things looked relatively normal. Except, the only traffic was an empty cross-sector 44 bus, which alarmed Apple. She looked down Park Heights and saw that people weren't on the bus and people weren't on the street either. Apple shook her head in disbelief concerned. Where were they, then? Sene was already up and she had found an old bamboo cutting board. She was practicing food alchemy, chopping, mixing and throwing things into a bowl. Talib woke up with a start. His mind was racing back to him. He watched Sene, he wanted to say, cooking, but saw no fire. "Where'd you get all that stuff from?"

"Your garden," Sene replied, returning to her work.

"My--? That stuff wasn't grown. It's only been a week."

"I thought you understood. Time is irrelevant. Intention is more important. Are you ready to break your fast? "

Looking quizzically at the bowl of food Sene handed him, Talib tried to recall the names for the vegetables. The big wrinkly green pieces were... "Kale, onion, cucumber, tomato." She pointed out each vegetable as he brought it up, examined it, and began to eat. "You don't know anything, do you?" "I just forgot," he snapped. "That's all." Sene smiled knowingly. This will pass soon. Talib returned her smile sheepishly. "I'm sorry. I'm...I'm still processing."

They ate together in silence. It had been too long since Talib had shared a meal with another person. He had nearly forgotten there ever was such a thing. It was comforting to have Sene there. It reminded him of his childhood. Still, with last night's conversation still bouncing around Talib's mind, he was more pensive than usual. "Thank you for the meal."

A slight nod of Sene's head put Talib at ease as he

prepared himself to leave for work. Dealing with Apple would need some careful planning. He decided to take the long way to work. Eyes skyward, he saw the satellite "Watcher" boards still listing alert status, illuminating the gray sky. Talib turned onto Narcissus, nearly crashing into a drone in search mode. It spun around just a few steps away from him, as if a gust of wind knocked it off course. He watched quizzically as the apprehending arms stretched out and clasped air before steering back to the stables. All the way across Belvedere Talib meditated on how limited the other people in his sector were by their chips. How outrageous it was he even lived in a sector. Everything was so manipulated and processed that it seems no one he knew had eaten fresh food in ten years. He was six or seven the last time he remembered peeling an orange, or eating any fruit that didn't have a shelf life of less than two years. People thought they were getting something good for them when all they were doing was slipping into darkness. Thanks, to Sene, it seemed Talib was the only one awake. It had to stop. Talib snapped to attention. He looked around in the street and didn't see any one else out. He didn't hear the normal street sounds. The concrete looked newly poured without and gang graffiti or footprints. Realizing he was alone, and that something was very unusual in the sector, he returned home. Sene was working in the garden, which he could see, was in full bloom. "What's happened to everyone?" Nonchalantly, Sene spoke and returned to her work, fine-tuning her new found dexterity by focusing on her hands' connection with the soil, "We've crossed the bummo."

"How? When?" Not turning to face Talib she said,

"There are some things you must learn here, before you are ready for the next step."

"Who's going to teach me?"

"I am."

"Then why did you let me go to the general store?" Sene turned watching him. Her gaze so stern he could feel her power as if she were trying to engrave the words in his brain. She finally spoke. "Talib, here is your first, and only, lesson. You choose your own reality."

ILE

BY KENISHA GROOMES-FAULK

Omi tutu...Cool Water.

From the water comes the beginning of everything.

I am young.

I am Black.

I am a female.

I grew up in the Inner City.

I grew up without a father.

My city had walls, boundaries, and borders.

But those walls were not marred by graffiti or murals to fallen souls.

My city had sidewalks, but no litter.

My city had limited access to the outside world, but not because politics or socioeconomics kept us apart from others.

Our boundaries kept us safe from the outside. We were trying to keep them OUT.

And those once on the inside, found guilty of the greatest offenses, were sent away. To the OUT. To a life of unimaginable, unspeakable horror.

My father was one of those that had been sent away.

I was determined to find him.

In the previous world, anyone who read my bio would think I was a statistic. In this world, that which did not kill those before me made me ...

Strong.

It was not a wonderful world outside anymore. The sky, so beautiful and blue in the archived portraits in the library, now held up an angry sun that burned our skin if we did not wear the appropriate protective clothing. We wore light and heat reflective uniforms, with long sleeves and pants, in the color scheme of the old U.S. military camouflaged fatigues. We wore lightweight helmets made of high impact absorption plastic, though the need to protect our heads from bullets, arrows, or stones was quickly becoming obsolete. Our helmets also housed frozen packets of gel coolant, offering 6 hours of cooling so that we would not overheat during longer excursions.

The air was hot and heavy and stagnant. Never a breeze. It was difficult to breathe, the stench of dead, dying, and drying plants, animals, and...people...was a new, macabre potpourri that greeted us when we stepped out of our armored vehicles. Street lights long burned out, and power lines without electrical currents pulsing through their interiors were strewn across the roads and walkways. Abandoned buildings, some gutted, some burned out, all greatly vandalized, stood defiantly against the decay, begging us, it seemed, to remember when they were beautiful. But we would not be deceived. You are not a home anymore, I imagine my chastisement would be. You are not a store. You are a corpse. Dead. Like everything and everyone outside of our walls.

We were paradise. They were paradise lost. It was hell on earth. Those of us that traveled outside, under heavy guard, were known as Angels. We brought hope. We brought life. We brought chance. And they wanted us to deliver. They wanted us for deliverance. Or they would want us for dinner.

I'm thankful for our city. I'm thankful for our elders. If it were not for them, we too would have been lost, left to fight for our lives against the dwindling resources of a dying planet. We knew that our city too, one day, would die. But we are the children of the ones who decided to do something about it before it was too late.

So many people thought 2012 was going to be the end-or beginning- of things. Nobody knew for sure what those things would be. Those that were afraid thought it would be the end of the world. That the God of heaven and earth would decide that it was time for things to end, and would either end the great life experiment after one last fight between his children, or that the universe itself, a powerful sentient being in and of itself would collapse under the weight of its own existence and start anew.

Then there were those who believed that nothing would happen except for a shift in awareness and consciousness, that the technology would dispel myth and humanity would evolve away from their superstitions, fear, and distrust of one another and move towards a more enlightened existence for all of mankind.

Finally, there were those who believed that nothing would happen except that which would be the result of whichever point on the spectrum had enough supporters and would, therefore, usher in the future they were collectively shaping through their politics, policies, religions, ideologies, and world views.

The elders of our community were those that belonged to the latter group and imagined a contingency for each scenario. They are the only reason we have survived as long as we have. Wars, famine, climate change, economic collapse, dwindling resources, then no resources were all waiting for us on the other side of 2012. But it wasn't 2012 that was the year of no return. It was actually 2015, and by 2028, what was once the campus of Morgan State University became our sanctuary.

Our community is called Ile. It means simply, Home.

Our elders were scientists, doctors, physicists, firemen, sanitation and transportation workers, as well as teachers, herbalists, chefs, psychologists, artists, martial artists, singers, dancers, painters. In the early days, there were accountants, but they quickly made use of their other skills. There were no politicians or bankers. There were spiritual people but no religious leaders. They simply were not consulted in the early days of the community's establishment, when the resources appeared to be plentiful, and the focus was on prosperity, not posterity. Our elders were selective, and they were quiet. There would be no more distractions.

At first, it was a few friends, a few families that came together at the first signs of society's change. The elections of 2008 and 2012, and every election thereafter, put leaders in office who were so controlled by corporate interests that ultimately the illusion of a separation between private industry and public office became nonexistent. As the earth's resources continued to dwindle and ecosystems collapsed, people began to leave the cities to the rising lawlessness. The fall was swift because all of the changes happened in rapid succession. We would not have to wait a thousand years to arrive at the place of no return. That time was the only reality most of us had ever known.

The first families quietly moved into place in a neighborhood on the East Side of Baltimore with small farms in Owings Mills, Maryland, relying on rations and small livestock. They were known as the "Walden Weirdo's", the

"Findhorn Folks", or the "Black Hippy Elite". Bur for the first time in the history of this country, here was a collective of Black Americans who did not feel the need to dispel myths or recruit members. It wasn't a mission, and there was no move to convert others to our way of life. They were simply preparing. And when the time arrived, to move the community to the next stronghold, the caravan of 7 families met with another caravan of 7 families, totaling 100 members, and moved onto the campus of the abandoned university.

In times of instability, culture is the first institution to be sacrificed. Schools at every level were hard to maintain, and eventually, unsafe to attend. Funding had long since dried up, and the homeless, desperate, and destitute had moved on to other points inside the city. Our elders and engineers had acquired and sectioned off three-fourths of the campus and erected a 20 foot wall around the entire parameter. In earlier days, the wall was an arrangement of booby traps, electrical wiring, short walls, and lookout posts. When the wars and riots rendered the United States a fractured union, it was the small communities that survived.

It is how we survived.

In the beginning, there were men and women. In the beginning, there was a word: harmony. Our elders believed that they would have a union of equality, balance, peace, and self-sustainability. There was no more social stratification. All were equal. There was no rich, there were no poor. There were leaders, and it consisted of the Elder Council, the original founders and visionaries of Ile. There were 5 men and 5 women.

At some point, though, the total distraction arose: hierarchy. Older versus younger. Man versus women. This was greatly distressing to the community who, growing ever aware of the world outside of our walls, did not want to see it come undone from within. That was when The Decision had to be made: the men of our community would no longer be able to hold a position on the council. Then the rise of the first coup nearly rendered the whole community obsolete. The weapons that were to be used for our defense were used in an attempt to seize power. But two of the women on the council, a psychologist and a data analyst, suspected the underpinnings of power were just beneath the surface, and secretly began monitoring and training a group of elite female soldiers to counter the threat.

Ile was shaken and nearly undone, and as punishment

for their offense, the men who took part in the rebellion, all men over the age of 18, had to leave the community. Sent outside of our walls without weapons, a few supplies, and whatever survival ability they brought with them. Some of their wives went with them, but the children would be allowed to stay. We would not let them take the children outside; knowing that without a safe house, supplies, or another community to join, they would be subjected to great suffering. This was a time of immense psychological trauma to the community. There were wives who remained, devastated by their husbands betrayal, shocked by the betrayal of the elders who did, after all, keep secrets. There were children separated from their parents. There were children who were taken by their parents before our walls were thoroughly fortified.

Testosterone was a problem. Hormones in general were a problem, and at the onset of puberty, our doctors began to monitor citizens. The men in our community were not allowed to join our armed forces, sentries, or anything that would incite them to violence. Our men were artists, philosophers, chefs. It was the women who policed the city, and eventually, began excursions to the surrounding cityscape in an effort to lead those left behind back to civilization.

It would take several generations for this to become the accepted standard of living. There were unions and family units. But the children were raised collectively. We were carried and nursed by our biological mothers, but all of the women of the community were our aunties, our other mothers. We knew who our fathers were, but every man was our father, our uncle, our brother. Our brothers were our brothers, our cousins were our cousins, our cousins were our brothers, our friends were our brothers, and our friends were our potential mates. But if you were female, you were simply SISTER.

We also frequently adopted rescued children into our community. Those were always interesting transitions, as we only brought in children who were infants up to the age of 12. No teenagers. And certainly no young adults. This was difficult, to see a person hungry, traumatized, on the verge of death, and not be able to help them. The elders were very clear: we have a maximum capacity. We shall not dishonor it as those in the outside world before us have done.

My mother is the youngest member of the Elder Council at 52 years of age. Typically, one did not become an Elder until they reached 65 years of age, but Mother had an uncanny presence and awareness about the future and safety of Ile that she was granted membership when she turned 50.

I was seven years old when my parents, along with other friends and colleagues, began planning for Ile. When I was 10 years old, we moved to the first safe community when it became unsafe for us to remain in Washington, DC. Initially planning to return to the deep south of North Carolina or even to leave for Brazil, they ultimately decided to partner with members of another collective who had the resources, wealth, means, and desire to transform Morgan State University into a sustainable community complete with solar energy, community farm, and a small scale city infrastructure. My education, along with the other children, to life in Ile, began immediately.

My mother carries with her memories of the earliest times, the successes, the failures, and the 'hard decisions' that had to be made. As such, the others defer to her authority and wisdom regarding difficult matters. She is the reason my cousin's request to rescue children from the outside world was granted. Before the war, he had been a child who required medical attention due to a complicated delivery, and could not bear to know that while we were safe inside our walls, that there were children being born on the outside who would be subject to all manner of atrocities. They were unthinkable, unspeakable. But we knew they were happening.

My mother was an artist, priestess, and acutely observant mind. She raised my sister, brother, and I to be leaders when one day I told her, 'mommy, I'm a leader, not a follower'. Her younger sister, the only member of her birth family to join her in Ile (before it was too late) and my cousin's mother, served as an advisor. She was very influential in the decision to continue rescuing the children from the outside. But we never took in their parents or their older siblings, and certainly never their men.

My father did not live with us in Ile anymore. I was not certain of the reason why my father had been sent away from the community, or if he left.   I knew him and enjoyed his company, his affection. Everyone called him Baba. He was quiet and well-read and taught Tai Chi and Yoga. He was also a musician who had been a martial artist before we came to live in Ile. The story goes that he began to question why men could no longer hold rights within Ile's council and that remaining within the walls would be our undoing, that we had to expand back outside our walls and begin to reclaim the area. We were going to quickly reach capacity within the city, which meant rescue excursions would have to be dramatically reduced. More and more outsiders were making their way to our parameter, having followed our armored trucks back to our compound, seeking entrance. The more they congregated near the parameter, the greater the threat of disease and possibly insurrection. To them, we were Noah's on the ark, refusing to open our doors to let them in from the flood.

"Nonsense", Mother would snap, her eyes narrowing and a frown creasing her forehead. "We made the difficult decisions. To be ridiculed, scorned, laughed at. For preparing for a disaster many believed would not come. They thought they were going to fly up into the sky before anything bad happened to them. That God would take them away from here. They thought us strange for our connection of politics, economics, science, and anything else they didn't understand. They had the same access to information, and they did not pay attention. When we built these walls and closed these doors, the ones who did not prepare had already begun to slip into an altered state. The city deteriorated into violence, murder, chaos, theft, rape, torture, and finally...cannibalism. It happened quickly, daughter, and we had to make a hard decision. We could not bring them in here. The toll of their trauma alone would have consumed a great deal of our resources. The security surrounding them would have been immense. And those that acquire a taste for human flesh...are no longer human. The older a child who survives out there, the more likely they have been subject to those conditions. They will be ill. They will be in a state between human and animal, and therefore unfit to live in this society. But the young ones that we find abandoned, the young ones who come to the collection centers...even the ones we have rescued from sacrifice, those about to be eaten by the insane and the desperate...are the ones where we place our hope. We can't save them all, but we can save who we can. And we can't save them at the sacrifice of ourselves. It is a hard decision, but it is the one that we make that has kept us here all this time".

I am one of the sentries. I travel outside of the walls of our city once a month to deliver packages of food and medicine at various safe points in the abandoned city where scavengers, some of them on their own, others in organized groups, pick up the supplies that ensure their survival. We deliver water purifying packets, donated clothing and shoes, and plants. From our farm, we collect seed, pot the plants, and when they begin to fruit, we deliver them to those we can with instructions on how to re-pot them and form their own gardens. So far, we are not aware of any communities banding together to replicate what we have done at Ile, but we know they are taking the supplies. When we drive out in our vehicles, the roads are pretty clear, and we are certain they are hiding as our security cameras can detect their movement around our parameter and our guards can see them. They know they are out-manned by the technology we have been able to hold onto. In the early days, there were attacks, but as the people grew weaker and sicker, they became content to scavenge and collect the supplies. Still, there were those on the outside that continued to prey on the less fortunate.

I never questioned the laws of Ile. As a child, we were all aware of the history that led to Ile's founding. What the world had been like and the corruption that made a city like ours necessary. Some cities were not as fortunate. Some people planned too late, if they planned at all, and many attempted to build anew using the paradigm of the old worldview. They imploded from within due to power struggles. They failed to diversify their population, and had too many with expertise in one field and none in the other. Many communities were undone by medical catastrophes, and others were walled in and trapped by their inability to grow food, preserve their numbers, or handle their waste properly.

From time to time and especially in the early days,

many of those who abandoned those cities   sought entrance into Ile, but all of them were turned away, except for the children under the age of 12.   It was difficult to watch our representatives communicate with those individuals at the outer wall plead their case for entry.   Many people showed up with children not their own in an attempt to garner pity and be granted entry.   When they would turn to leave, our sentries would stop them and take the children.   Some fought, others did not.   Early on, the elders learned the importance of scanning for weapons after a man pulled out a gun and murdered his entire family upon being denied entry into the city.   His madness and grief had reached its limit. Mother had warned the council that such a measure was necessary, and while they agreed, the scanner had malfunctioned.   If it had worked properly that day, the children would have been granted entrance and the adults left outside.   The threat of collusion was too great a risk to take.

The outsiders were growing sicker and weaker and were not as great a threat as they had been once upon a time. There was a time when they were incredibly violent, when weapons were still accessible.   Earlier units, decades before, reported grotesque scenes of societal collapse on the streets of Baltimore city.   It was images straight from nightmares, and many of our finest soldiers left the force after that.   The psychologists had special treatment for those who witnessed and interrupted such atrocities, or those that had to engage in combat with others.

I volunteered for this service because I was intent upon finding my father. Though I understood the need to preserve the Ile, he was my father. I couldn't believe he would set out to bring down Ile. I couldn't. My mother and I were estranged over the matter because she never showed any emotion when speaking about him. There were many women like her in Ile. Between their generation and mine, there was an overpowering sense of disconnect regarding the operations of our community. I didn't understand how you could love someone, have children with them, and not fight for them when they have been condemned to certain death. Unless she believed he was guilty.

And I just could not believe that.

Ori tutu...Cool Head.

May the choices we act upon be reflective...and wise.

Today something happened that I wasn't expecting.

My team of six sentries inside our armored truck and two car escorts, one in the front, one in the back, composed of ten well trained women, came upon the shock of our life. We delivered our usual packages of 5 potted plants, a large box of clothing, a box of medical supplies, water purification packets, and dehydrated food packets when a girl came running out of trees towards us. She had a backpack that she clutched close to her, her filthy clothes in tatters, her hair matted and wild. She was running, panting, and crying, and Zen, one of our lookouts spotted her as soon as she broke the tree line. Nanyun, my partner, raised her weapon as the others shouted for her to drop her package and freeze. She began to scream and kept running. It was then that I noticed a group of men were running behind her, and if she stopped, I could only imagine what would happen to her.

"Stand down!" I yelled to my team, motioning for them to move into formation. The men chasing the girl saw us, and some of them slowed down. One of them had a bow and arrow and raised it, preparing to shoot the girl. Without a thought, I raised my gun and fired a single shot, striking him in the head. We were taught never to shoot to maim. You shoot to kill. Another man with a long knife, sped up around his friend, prepared to throw the knife at the girls back when Anansa fired her weapon. I prayed none of them had a gun before we would be able to reach the girl.

"Stop where you are!" I yelled.

"You are outnumbered and out gunned! Leave with your lives NOW!" The men slowed their run, as a couple began assessing their fallen comrades. They lifted them by arms and legs and carried them off as a couple looked angrily at us and stared longingly at the girl that continued to make her way across the grass towards us. Turning, they ran back to their group. I shuddered to think about what they would do to the bodies.

She was almost to us, and I could hear her panting and see the fear in her wide eyes. She looked to be approximately 15 years old and was very, very thin. I could tell she was starving, but she had the strength to run nearly at the speed of light, clutching her bag to her chest. Once she reached us she began to scream and cry, and collapsed in front of me.

My team moved in protective formation around me and the girl as I moved towards her, with my weapon pointed at her, to begin contact. "PUT THE BAG DOWN AND YOUR HANDS UP! HANDS UP! PUT YOUR HANDS WHERE I CAN SEE THEM!" She continued to cry and shake, clutching her bag, eyes closed. Slowly she put her bag down and raised her hands, slowly. She was shaking so hard I thought her bones would break from the violent vibrations. She looked at me, and I could see bruises on her face. I could smell the stench of unwashed blood, sweat, and filth on her.

Suddenly I heard a soft cry coming from the bag.

A baby. She had a baby in the bag.

After we'd assessed that the girl had no weapons, we put her in the truck with us and left. We drove towards one of the safe houses on the way back to our city where we would be safe and could question her more thoroughly. I could feel the eyes of my team on me, and I knew that at least one of them, Anansa, would not be happy about bringing an outsider into our vehicle and safe house.

We entered the code, entered through the gate, and pulled up to the front door. Once we were inside and the area was secure, I began looking over the girl. She was still shaking, looking at us with fear and relief, clutching the baby close to her chest.

"Who are you?" I asked her as gently as I could.

"Kory", she whispered.

"Kory, what were you doing out there all alone today, and with a baby? That was pretty dangerous, you know".

"I know, but I had...had to get away from that place. Quinn told me...he told me today was the day the Angels came to drop off the pots. He told me if he didn't come back, to go to the spot where the Angels come and wait for them in the trees because they would help me. Those other men...they heard me moving around, and they started chasing me. I was...I was so scared...Quinn didn't come back...they got him...they got him..."

I looked at the ladies on my team. Two were at the front door; two were at the back door. The other six stayed in circle formation around me and Kory, weapons lowered. I could see Anansa's eyes narrowing as the girl spoke. I would deal with her later.

"Kory, whose baby is this?" She pulled the baby to her chest, her arms wrapped so tight she was hugging herself.

"He's mine."

"Kory, this baby looks like he's only a couple of days old. When did you have him?"

She stared at me with large, frightened eyes. "I had him three days ago. Quinn left to find some water, we ran out, and I got a fever. He said if he didn't come back to make sure I got to the field, that the Angels would find me and the baby. He said you would take my baby so nobody would eat him. He said...you might take me too...cuz I'm only 12".

My God...

"Sarge...we have a problem. We can't take that girl back. She's too old. And we were ordered not to seek out any more refugees. The city is not producing as much food as we need for those that we have, we can't afford to bring more people and continue the food and supply drops." This from Anansa, who followed orders to the letter during any assignment.

"Anansa...I'm not leaving her. Did you hear what she just said? She has a newborn baby, three days old. She is all alone out here now, a 12 year old with a dead lover. She was being chased by a group of men who would have tortured her, raped her and her baby, and killed them both. There is no way I am turning either one of them away."

"Sarge, I have it from the authority of the council to deliver our packages and return without any refugees".

"I will deal with The Council when we get back. I'm not leaving either one of these children out here".

Silence. She was pissed. But she would not challenge me while we spoke in whispers in a corner of the room. Our medic, Adwoa, was assessing the baby and Kory and our communications specialist, Nailah, used the radio to dispatch back to headquarters that we would be returning with two refugees, both within the accepted age of reception. When instructed to leave the package and the children by order of the Council, she simply handed the radio to me.

"This is Sergeant Strong. I am requesting to bring these children to the inner walls for medical treatment. It is not safe out here for them, both of them are under the age of Divine Protection, and we cannot leave them here. Take this message to the Council and have a cabin prepared for us". With that, I handed the radio back to Nailah and walked away to prepare to transport our group back to our vehicles.

We had been in the safe house for over 10 minutes, too long to be out of our vehicles, though we had sentries outside, still...if there were men watching us, they would be tempted to try to attack us.

"Alright everyone, it is time to move out. Let's go!"

Motion. Like a well oiled machine, two soldiers in the front, two in the back, and the remainder formed a circle around me, Kory, and the Baby, with Anansa covering them within our circle as we exited the house and re-entered our vehicles. Curled up in her filthy clothes and a small blanket in the truck, Kory sat still and silent, watching all of us with a mixture of joy and fear on her face. I didn't want to imagine what her life had been like on the Outside. If she was indeed 12 years old, that meant she was born in 2016, one year after the Great Collapse.

Everything fell so quickly that what scientists and analysts thought would take many generations to take place occurred within the short span of five years. By year ten following the fall, manufacturing and production had all but halted. The wealthy shut themselves up in enclaves, using their influence and wealth to distance themselves from the world outside their bubble. We had a bubble too, but ours was a bubble of survival, built by those who could continue the work for the community and not rely on the work of others to get what we needed, because we knew it would never come. The poor continued to be exposed to the elements, the police crackdown and the fallout of the war. We were thankful that Baltimore was spared the fallout from the war, but the surrounding cities were not so lucky. We think our proximity to Fort Meade played a big part in Baltimore not suffering more damage than it did. But still, the total absence of any sort of government or organized infrastructure allowed lawlessness to take over pretty quickly. I don't know where the others went, and we never communicated with any of the other communities that might be like Ile. I think The Council wanted to change that.

We pulled up to the south side of Ile, what had been the service roads for delivery trucks to bring supplies to the campus during it's time as a school. There were people, children, tents, carts, and other evidence of the refugee city that was forming along the outside parameter of Ile. There were men but mostly women and children. We gathered that most of these men were the fathers, husbands, brothers, cousins, or friends of women and children gathered there to make sure they reached the city safely. By now, everyone knew that Ile did not accept outside men and women. Sometimes, parents lied about their children's ages, to make them appear younger than 12. With the amount of malnutrition and psychological trauma, many children were no larger or intelligent than a 12 year old anyway. And we still could not take them.

To test the true age of a child in question, we relied on dental exams. Our dentist took an x-ray of the teeth and compared it to the archived records we had on file. We did not accept or consider birth certificates because the risk of forgery was guaranteed.

We pulled safely through the gate and watched it close behind us. Thankful for the solid iron wall obstructing us from the wretched souls outside, we exited the truck with the children. We had a few cabins set up in this space between the outer and inner walls, where those who were approved to seek entrance waited. We would not allow men to enter this area anymore, so women with children, or groups of children with older women would wait here with them, where they would receive food and clean water, bathe, and the most basic of medical treatment. During this time, the Council and the advisors would consider each case, paying close attention to the child's age, medical condition, and analysis of stool sample. If human remains were found in young children, we would not take them, as the danger of prion related illness was too risky. That had been the case more than any of us cared to realize, and the decision to send a young child beyond the outer wall was always nearly impossible. The cries, the screams, the pleading is not something one should ever get used to.

One of the reasons for our excursions was to establish a community of those denied entrance into Ile but well enough to maintain and establish their own safe community as an extension of Ile. We needed to be certain Ile could be sustained 20 years after its founding before we'd think of branching out. Because our supplies were now meeting the limit of our population, we needed to move from the idea to the institution. But this was a closely guarded secret as well, because we could not risk rumor from the outside world impending progress.

Rain, my aunt, met me at the security doors to the examination room. She ordered the staff to take Kory, and the baby to be further assessed, bathed, clothed, and fed, never taking her eyes off me. I knew she was here in place of my mother, and I knew my mother was not happy with me.

"I need a word with you in private, Strong…"

"Rain, I know, but let me just…"

"AUNT RAIN, young lady, don't you DARE call me by my first name right now. As a matter of fact, Advisor Renier will be even better. Come…with…me".

I followed my aunt to the conference room where the speaker phone was set up. My mother was elsewhere in Ile, most likely in the administrative building with the rest of the council. It was always difficult for me to confer with my mother over the phone because I could not see her face. Right now, I didn't want to see it, but I needed to see it in order to determine how deeply she felt about not having these children under these circumstances. I decided to speak first.

"Advisor Renier, please, with all due respect..."

"Stop it Strong, just stop it! With all due respect, you are a little late in considering due respect. The Council SPECIFICALLY said no more refugees right now. Your mother SPECIFICALLY instructed you, no more refugees right now. And I know Anansa reminded you of our protocol. Strong, you can NOT draw attention to your affiliation with high ranking members of The Council. You are the child of a Founding Member AND a Council Member, the youngest council member in our history. Do NOT make any of us regret allowing your mother that privilege and you this opportunity. NO MATTER WHAT!"

"Renier, it CAN'T be an issue of NO MATTER WHAT! Did you see that girl? She's 12...with a baby. It wasn't that long ago that something like that would have made you flinch in disbelief. I saw a 12 year old GIRL running for her life and for the life of a BABY from a group of about 25 men who were set on doing everything under the sun to her and that child BEFORE they would have been merciful enough and just killed them. Do you honestly think I would have dropped off a care package, a note, and said 'Good Day' to all of them? The care package be damned, today we actually saved a life!"

Aunt Rain slammed her hand down on the table, and for the first time, I noticed the conference button flicker. It was on the whole time. Mother was here. Silent. Listening.

"DO YOU KNOW HOW MANY TIMES I HAVE HEARD SIMILAR STORIES, STRONG?! How many groups of children, all under the age of protection, found by sentries, only to be left behind? Yes, with our packages, and instructions. Our sentries return and find the children gone or murdered? Yours is not the first young mother and child to be found but dammit Strong, if you START this, you will have on your head the burden of THE LAST rescued children allowed to come into Ile. We just can NOT do this right now!"

"THEN WHY ARE WE DOING THESE DROPS?! WHAT IS THE PURPOSE IN SAVING PEOPLE IF WE ARE NOT REALLY SAVING THEM?!"

"We do the best we can, Strong". My mother finally speaks. "We do what we can, when we can, how we can. And we leave the rest to fate. It is the best we can do".

"Mother...how can we leave children defenseless out there? It happened right in front of us, what should I have done, ordered my team to kill the men, give the girl the box, and send her in the opposite direction? It would have been better to have put a bullet in them both than to do that".

Silence.

"Oh, I can't believe this", I groaned. "Are you serious? Mother, is this really where we are? Why are we delivering packages if this is the reality now?"

"If you see a group of men chasing an unarmed woman, yes, you kill them. If they are near any of our safe houses or drop off points, they are a threat, and should be neutralized. If you believed they would have tortured and murdered her, yes, you should have killed them. Because that is what Angels do: they bring a message of hope and deliverance, even to those desperate to hang onto the hell of their lives, with a message of death. I thought you understood this when we allowed you command of your own team. You have trained for this. What is the difference now?"

"She didn't join The Sentry just to be an Angel, Nia. She's looking for Kofi".

Kofi...my father. I didn't doubt for one moment Rain

would know this, or my mother. I didn't expect it to be an issue now, because these were two separate issues in my mind.

"Rain, that has nothing to do with this…"

"You do not deny that you are looking for your father, Strong?"

"Mother, I don't think this is the time for this conversation."

"It is if you are LOOKING to save someone because you could not save your father. Under any other circumstance, you would have been within your power to eradicate that threat, deliver the package to the girl, and direct her, or even transport her to another settlement that we KNOW is safe. You did not have to bring her here. Explain yourself".

I had not thought of sending her to one of the other less organized and protected settlements at all. I had not even entertained the topic with my team, who I am sure wondered the same but would not have questioned my decision in the field. I didn't want to do that for one simple reason: I had not found my father. In the six years that I had been training and eventually advancing to head up my own team I had not found my father. I had not seen him since I was 12 years old, and when I saw Kory, I saw myself, and in that baby boy, I saw the hope of finding my father. A male that I could bring back home. I didn't even know if my father was alive, but in an instant, I saw a way to bring the idea of my father back home.

I didn't realize how convoluted things would become. My mother and aunt did, however.

"Advisor Rain, please have the members of Angel Team 5 complete their debriefings and handle the preliminary report on these children. We expect an update in the morning, per standard protocol. Strong...I will see you at home."

Ile tutu...Cool Home.

May the home be filled with love, and protected from all negative forces.

Always.

My cousin Naveen came to visit me today with an update on Kory and the baby. He was one of our most prominent students in the field of neuroscience in Ile and worked closely with his mother, Renier, a psychologist, in assessing refugees. Their trauma would be our work if we were not careful and not aware. For all it was worth, he thought I made the right decision. The Council was furious, and I was being summoned to their chambers, which was the first step in public discipline. The community deserved to know whenever there were threats to our governance, and in my act of charity, I had threatened to undermine the stability and future of our community. My team had given their statements, and though I'm not sure what was said, I'm certain that even in their neutrality my actions stood in stark contrast to the leadership that was expected from me. I know that if anybody tried to advocate for me, it would be Zen.

I waited alone in the quarters I shared with my mother. My brother and sister lived with their own families, and our units were situated next to one another, as most families remained in close proximity to one another. Living with my mother was strained because of the answers she would not give us regarding our father, but I had learned to live in the moment of our relationship, for what it was worth, for what it was. Today would be the test of all of that.

I was sitting in the kitchen sipping a glass of mint

water when my brother and sister entered our unit. I could tell by the look on their faces that they knew what happened during my excursion, and I knew they were here to be a part of the discussion with mother before we went before the council and the community. I could tell by the look on my sister's face that things were not going to be in my favor. And knowing this, I still felt a sense of detached calm, because I could not conceive of what everybody feared.

Banishment; for saving a life? For saving children's lives?

My brother, Paz, came over and put an arm around my shoulders, kissing the side of my head. "Strong...Strong... Strong...what have you done, girl?" He sighed. My brother was an artist, a painter, and a Tai Chi master. He was always quiet and observant, and usually when he spoke, he always had something profound to say, even when he was joking. He and I were closer in age than my sister and I, and I was closer to him in maturity, but I was also close to my sister, Amor, being that we were girls with similar interests. Plus, Amor knew my reasons for becoming a sentry, and supported my endeavors, albeit secretly. The redness in her eyes told me she had been crying for me, and I just hugged her tightly, her tears wetting her cheeks and mine.

"Well good, you are all here, saves me from having to

repeat this information more than once. Come with me, all of you," mother directed as she entered the room. I froze at the sound of her voice; I could hear her resolve but also her weariness. All because of me.

We walked to her study and took a seat. We rarely entered this room, this was mother's space. There were pictures of us, pictures of Ile members, but no pictures of my father.

Nobody spoke, but as we sat before mother's desk, Paz and Amor took my hands, and squeezed them. We had not had to sit like this for years...not since we were informed that our father was leaving and that he was not coming back. Ever.

What had I *done*?

"As you all know, we had a situation yesterday involving your sister. Against the Council's command to not bring back refugees, Strong decided to bring a young mother and her child to Ile. I am going to tell it to you straight: we are officially at maximum capacity and within the next 24 hours will effectively shut down our Free Zone until further notice. The outer parameter will need to be cleared and expanded. Supply drops will continue for another month while we assess how, and if we will be able to move forward."

"Strong, when you broke the rules, you put us in a difficult position where we now have to explain to the members of Ile where we stand with our supplies, our food, and our future. These two children have anchored a very real conversation that we have been trying to figure out for some time now. We simply cannot bring in more people, we are full. We have been full, which is why we began to use the drops as more than just charity. They are outreach. They are reconnaissance. We have been trying to seed other communities so that we can expand and form a network of communities in order to rebuild with the outside world."

"As you are aware, your father was sent away from Ile because he and others felt strongly that our system of governance would lead to our demise. Those that left with him and those that remained were very sharply divided on this issue, and an Ile divided cannot stand. However...all that you have heard about that time is not the full truth."

"Your father helped found Ile. And when the decision was made to remove men from the Council, your father did not agree, but he understood that, in times like these, we needed to draw on our strengths and adapt. Around this time, his sister, her husband, and their four children from

North Carolina made it to Ile, the only members of their family to make it this far north. All of them, except for the youngest, were beyond our age of acceptance into Ile. We were faced with the decision of turning away our own family. It was the hardest decision your father ever made. The Council had to be unbiased and unwavering in establishing the laws for Ile: no adult members. No men. No children older than 12. It was law, and it could not be undone. Your father was given a choice: stay in Ile with his own family, or allow the youngest one to stay in his place."

"Together, we made a decision. We decided that he, and a few of the others, would leave Ile with the intention of establishing a sister community amongst the refugees, among them his own family members who could not be brought into Ile. I would stay here and raise the three of you from within the safety of our walls. We had to keep this secret, we could not allow word to get out that another community was forming, where it would be, or how it would be stocked because we could not risk sabotage, theft, robbery, or anything that would impede progress. It is very dangerous out there; Baltimore is not the city we all remembered. We grow our food here in greenhouses, but the soil on the outside is depleted and getting worse every year. There is very little wildlife, and clean water is very difficult to access. Your father was one of the few men trained to deal with that sort of terrain and the ability to transform what he could find into something sustainable. We cannot deal with all of the survivors, but he could, we hoped."

"The Council is aware of our goal to expand Ile. They are not aware though that within the Council is another, smaller Council, who has already put those plans into place. The Council has a 20 year vision, but we realized that we needed to fast track that vision as soon as possible. It is the only reason we have been able to live in security and relative normalcy. That normalcy is precious to us, and it is what has allowed us to help the world around us and within our walls rebuild."

"Your father has been sending word to us through some of the children we have taken in over the years. And I have been in communication with him. I do miss him, terribly. But to protect the secrecy of the work he must do, we could not allow anyone, not even his children, to know where he was or what he was doing. I have always told you that he loved you very much, but I could not and would not say more."

"But mother, you let us believe he was a traitor..." Amor interrupted, the weight of her hurt hanging heavily around her words.

"And in that belief I did everything I could to make sure you knew in your heart of hearts that he loved you more than anything, but that you had to be okay with decisions that were beyond your control. If your father had been a traitor, would you walk around with the shame and stigma of his choices on your head? No, I raised you to face your fears and hurts head on and to put them to rest so that they did not motivate or control you."

"Kory was sent to us by your father. The name Quinn she used was a coded message to me. I used to call your father The Mighty Quinn when we first met. It was his way of letting me know that he was sending these children to us. He sent them as a way of letting us know that he is still out there, doing the work. He is bringing order out there, but it's still not safe enough for the children he finds."

I sat there. Silent. Processing all of this information, rolling every word over in my mind. My father was alive. Out there. In that cruel world, he was a hero. He was a savior. He was a leader, and he was doing the work of Ile in a way that nobody could have imagined. He braved the apocalypse. And he did it alone.

Mother's voice snapped me out of my moment of relief and release. "And now, Strong, you are going to face a difficult decision of your own. We are shutting down the food drops and instituting a one child per family rule. That means our own Ile members will be limited to one child in order to not tax the remaining resources that we have, until such a time as we are able to expand and increase production. In order for Kory and the baby to stay, you must give up your right to your own future children...or you will have to leave. If you stay, Kory and her child will become your children, but you will not be able to have any of your own. You will also be stripped of your post as commander of Angel Team 5. If you leave, they will remain and grow up under our protection but will be placed with two separate families. Nobody can parent a 12 year old who is a parent herself."

She paused, and I realized that she said these words without pause or hesitation, until her voice cracked. I looked up to see that she was crying...tears...running down her face. My mother, the strong and stoic one. She looked and sounded so broken.

"Strong...baby...you have to *go*."

The room went dark around me as mother pre-sentenced me on behalf of the Council. I couldn't see her, the room, or hear my brother and sister beyond the gasps that sucked the air out of the room and my lungs. I could only hear the pulsing, pounding, thump of the blood pumping through my veins, in sync with my beating heart. The icy cold grip of fear snaked its way up my spine, raising the hairs on the back of my neck, and I shuddered. My eyes closed.

Finally…I exhaled…

The sound filled the room with a voluminous explosion. Paz was on his feet yelling at mother, asking her how could she let them hand down such a harsh sentence. Amor had wrapped her arms around me, crying, shaking her head no, and pleading with mother to have mercy and to not let this happen. Mother sat at her desk, her face a blank slate of emotion. Mother wore the mask very well. She told me that for the majority of her youth, she existed in an emotional state, and felt the weight of every moment of pain, fear, joy, happiness, and anger. It was exhausting and interfered with her personal development, she felt. "Take nothing personal, not even the good that others do to you", she would tell me. This was not personal.

So those were my choices. Stay in Ile, stripped of my title, without a job but with two children to raise and the inability to ever have my own biological children one day. Or leave Ile and join my father, who I had not seen in over a decade, in a foreign and violent world.

I feel numb.

I feel confused.

I *am* afraid.

It is said that when Oduduwa, the progenitor of the Yoruba people, left Egypt, his father asked the spirits-the Orisha- to travel with and protect him.

When he arrived on the west coast of Africa, he established the Yoruba nation. He left alone, but from him, came many.

My ancestors were taken from their land, crossed the Atlantic ocean to the Caribbean, the America's, and Europe. Stripped of their cultural and spiritual identities, through many generations, until one day, someone, somewhere, remembers. They gather the people together, and bring back the customs and traditions.

These are what has kept us and made us strong. This history is why we were prepared for the worst while we lived the best way we knew how.

And now, I am leaving my people. I am leaving my
home. I am leaving my identity behind. I faced my Council
Elders and my community, and accepted their decision. Kory
and her son, Agyei, whose name means 'Messenger of God' in
the Akan language of Ghana, took my place in Ile. They were
kept together, but eventually they would be placed with other
families so that Kory's healing from her trauma would be
more complete. She was just 12 years old, after all...

I said my goodbyes. Mother walked me to the outer
gates, along with the members of Angel Team 5, escorting us
in one final show of solidarity masked as security detail.
Mother held my hand tightly. As she hugged me for the final
time, my sobs ripped from my belly, and I held onto her to
keep from drowning in my fear. She whispered in my ear:

"Oduduwa was not alone. And neither are you. Baba
is waiting for you, Baby Girl. See?"

She pointed to the end of the road, which had been
cleared of refugees. No men, no women, no children; just
dirt, dried patches of grass and trees.

He stepped from behind the tree, and raised his arm
with a closed fist.

My mother wrapped her arms around me once again,

and then clutched her hands to her heart. I took my steps away from her, the way I did when I first learned to walk, and stumbled my way to my father, tears blurring my vision. I reached him, and noticed...his face was still...my face.

"Baby Baby-Girl", he said softly, and hugged me. And held me. I held him back, and then we began walking away. I looked over my shoulder, once again, at my home.

I vowed that one day, we would all be together again.

Ase, Ase, Ase o...

THE DEBT

BY MIRLANDE JEAN-GILLES

The early morning air was already sooty and thick. Dark clouds of smog and smoke billowed in the brightening sky over the city. Samia Apacou was riding her hovee at minimum speed with the other rush hour motorists going down the I-83 in Old Baltimore. She was upset and needed to get away right then. She screamed inside her helmet and in a burst of speed she escaped from the pack. They were all heading into the city to work. Old Baltimore had the most debt camps and the least citizens actually living there. Samia took hair-pin turns at top speed, cut vehicles off and tailgated. Samia's cousin Noel worked at the debt camp with her. He was not far behind, trying to catch up. He was upset. He understood Samia's rage, but she was being reckless. For Samia, speeding felt good. The force of the wind pushing against her cleared her mind. She couldn't focus on anything but controlling the fast moving, shuddering vehicle. She got off at her regular exit in West Baltimore to wait for her cousin. It was a restricted zone, but the gate was always unlocked and the barricades were easy to maneuver around.

Except for the music of the birds and crickets in the overgrown grass, the streets were quiet and abandoned. Some of the once quaint, brick row houses had entire facades crumbled at their stoops in surrender to the elements. Houses that were standing were in disrepair. Their once closed rooms were exposed like doll house insides. Some of the three story buildings stood fully robed in pleats of vines that completely veiled them.

Samia took off her helmet. The air was thick and she coughed a few times. Her seething anger had calmed to an aching, helpless madness. She got off the steaming, clicking vehicle. She tried to catch her breath as she leaned against a large tree whose roots had pushed open the sidewalk. She closed her eyes listening to the whistles, chirps and songs of many birds. Their beautiful melodies distracted her for a moment, but too many bad things were crowding her mind.

Her heartbeat would not slow down.

A text the night before let her know that because of her recent father's imprisonment she would have to work off part of his debt. Prisoner's work did not go towards their debt. His debt was to be distributed to his family and his five kids. Samia was on the final year of her debt. She heard Noel's hovee before she saw it. He was pissed and didn't even want to look at her. He let his hovee fall onto the crumbling concrete sidewalk when he got off. He took off his helmet and tossed it near the hovee. He was shaking. As he walked up to Samia he said, "I understand what you're going through, but what you just did was so reckless! Your foolishness is gonna get you hurt." His voice echoed down the empty blocks. "I was so pissed! I just wanted to get away," Samia said. She knew how stupid it sounded, but she had no excuse. She wasn't thinking.

"You're risking everyone's life." Noel said through his teeth.

Samia responded with a sudden cloudburst of tears. She said, "It's so unfair." She sniffled and couldn't go on. For Noel, seeing his cousin cry made his anger dissipate just like that. It shook him up 'cause she was always the strong one. "I can't believe after busting my ass all these years...working since I was eleven years old... determined not to spend my life in debt. I gave my childhood." Her throat was so dry.

Samia has worked since she was a child to pay off her personal, federal and family debt. Working took priority over schooling. She took classes online which satisfied the requirements for a diploma. Samia was just twenty-three years old and her shoulders were rounded downward, her spine already curved. The years of toiling in debt camp factories shaped her, aged her. Noel put his hand on his cousin's shoulder.

"Sam, I'm so sorry that it happened like this. You are the hardest worker out there and this is just wrong."

"I was done. I mean this was my last year. They yank me back in like this? My father is nothing to me. He has five kids and not one of us knows him well enough to call him daddy." Samia's biological father got around the "two children per family" law by having children with multiple women, but he could not provide child support to any of them. He was going to prison for a series of burglaries, squatting, and robbery. She wasn't sure how many years he was getting, but she knew three of his years were now hers. He would be used as a migrant worker to pick corn, cotton and other crops.

Noel's personal messaging device beeped. He was glad for the distraction because he had no idea what to do or say to help. He checked his text while his cousin blew her nose and wiped her red eyes.

"Let's get going." Noel walked to his hovee very concerned that if they didn't get walking they would be late.

"We're gonna be late, Sam."

"Who cares if we're late! Who gives a got damn!" Samia shrieked. She threw her helmet to the ground. The loud clunking reverberated off the buildings and echoed down the streets. Small rodents scurried deeper into their underground burrows.

"Come on Sam," Noel said. Samia had her arms crossed stubbornly she shook her head and picked up her helmet. She knew things could not go on the way they had been. She went over to her hovee. They didn't ride them because they wanted to talk. Instead, they walked along with them like kids pushing their bikes. The two of them were nondescript in tan debt camp work jumpsuits. The sound of their work boots thumped on the concrete. Samia had drawn peace signs, ankhs and hearts on hers even though the symbols were illegal.

People squatted in the decent row houses. They watched Samia and Noel as they walked by. The families farmed in the lots, ignoring the government's no grow laws. The cousins walked by a lot with corn growing on golden and green stalks taller than them. The leaves rustled as a sulfur smelling breeze blew. The cousins hadn't noticed all the birds had stopped squawking and singing.

The hawk was almost silent as it swooped down, and quickly snatched up a small rodent from the lot. It was gone quickly and quietly with dinner in its beak. Nature in all her cruel beauty was before them.

"Wow!" Samia marveled. "Whoa," Noel said with surprise. They started walking.

"I'm going to splish!" Samia blurted out. She couldn't keep it in anymore.

"Splish? To where? Only richies can get passports."

Noel felt a sudden clench in his gut. He didn't like where their conversation was going.

"I'm not trying to move richie-style. I would let the waters of life move me," Samia said wistfully.

"Where would you go? South? West? There's so much water out there."

"Noel, beyond our vision there are other worlds." Samia looked at him and then whispered the word, "Providence".

Noel shook his head trying to deflect her words. He felt almost sick at how dangerous what she was saying was. His heart was pounding. His reaction was counted on. The population was being bombarded by subliminal and not so subliminal messages that affirmed loyalty to the Debt. He couldn't believe Providence could exist.

"You've got to keep your head about you. Where is all

this coming from anyways?" Noel said a bit harshly. "You're talking about a free land where there are no camps, no debt to pay and folks just live? People farm the land without harassment? A place like that would have been busted long ago."

"It exists. It's real. Online, I keep getting the end of threads about it. They keep shutting down the sites that talk about it, but on the boards folks can speak more freely..."

Samia said quietly. They pushed through some thick brush that shielded some gates. The locks had been broken long ago and the cousins walked out of the restricted zone. They were getting closer to their work building so they said nothing else because the area was being monitored.

Even before the mess with her father's debt Samia had been thinking about Providence. There was a quiet movement building toward freedom. Samia knew she needed a ship to get there and that it was north. They knew so much less because of how much their internet was censored. On map apps, entire countries were removed, history rewritten, world news censored. Libraries were one of the first places shut down to the public when the new government took over.

Noel and Samia turned the corner where their plain, concrete work building was situated. A large sign written in Mandarin and English identified the plant's number and name. The United States was ruled and its' doings were dictated by Chinese interests and money. The real China, where dissidents were killed, intellectuals jailed, all media censored and population controlled. Only two kids were allowed per American family. The tremendous calamities of 2012 completely collapsed the world's economies. The earthquakes, meteor hits, hurricanes and tornadoes pummeled cities all over the world. The natural disasters destroyed infrastructure, governments leaving many countries vulnerable and needy. Though China suffered too, they still had power, money and a large military.

Other hovees and road cars were parked in front of their factory. The cousins walked towards the building quietly. As they parked their hovees, Samia had the urge to run. There were other workers going inside the building too. Samia and Noel waited behind them as they went through their check-in procedures at the front desk. Everyone was solemn. Samia watched as the round, little, silver PIDs with their beady, red laser eye came out of their wall units and floated over to scan the workers. The PIDs checked their temperatures, blood pressure and heart rates. PID was short for Personal Interface Device. The PID could tell if the worker needed to use the bathroom, it could even x-ray and detect weapons. Samia was close to the edge as the PID swooped over to her.

It was so invasive. Samia wasn't supposed to, but she crossed her arms over her chest and held up her head as if the whole thing smelled. The PID transmitted her out of control vitals to the computer terminal on the desk where a guard sat reading everyone's biological business. All Noel could do was look and send peaceful thoughts to his cousin. He saw the anger in her set jaw and clenched fists. As the PID hovered near her cramping abdomen the guard looked up and smiled wickedly at her.

"You should go change your tampon," he sneered.

Without thinking and fueled by anger she smashed the PID at the guard like a tennis player smashing a 100 MPH ball back at her opponent. The guard ducked quickly and the PID hit the wall behind him with a terrible crunch.

"No Sam!" Noel yelled too late.

Everyone gasped and stepped back. It was silent for just a moment as all eyes stayed on the dead, little electronic PID on the ground. Noel ran over to Samia.

"Sam! What the hell?" Noel had fear in his eyes. Samia just stood there in disbelief. The desk guard was up and cursing at her in Mandarin. The guard then knelt in front of the broken PID. Unmarked doors flung open and the lobby was filled with armed security guards. They surrounded Samia and the biggest female one grabbed her arm tightly.

"Get off me!" Samia struggled. And the guard pulled out her baton and threatened Samia with it.

"Stop! Leave her alone!" Noel yelled. He was forcibly held back and then herded out of the lobby with the other shocked workers. The check-in guard carefully held the smashed PID like it was a baby bird. He laid it on his desk. They threw Samia in a windowless, empty office and locked her in. She sat slouched in front of a desk that had no papers or anything on it. She was so upset and disappointed at herself at first. And then gradually she calmed down. Being in the room gave her time to think. Even though she was scared because she knew they were calculating her cost for the damage, she found comfort in thinking about what Providence might be like. She imagined waking up and being a free woman. It made her feel strong, it made her feel like there was more to life than she ever imagined.

They told her in a text that six months would be added to her debt time. As soon as she read it someone unlocked the door and it opened it, but they did not go into the office. Samia just sat there numb and staring at her PMD. Six months?

"Get out," a voice demanded. It surprised and jolted Samia. She scrambled up and wiped her eyes. As she was walking out the door she realized it didn't matter how much time they gave her Providence was there like a golden, shining beacon pulling her out of her doldrums. A guard told her to get back to work. As she made her way to her workstation the workers stared. She was calm, but would not look up at anyone. Samia was known as a good worker who sometimes spent weeks in the debt camp dorms, not going home at all. She would sleep in the dorms for a few hours after work and then would wake up, eat and then return to work.

There were workers who didn't have a place to live, they could not afford rent. The tiny stipends they received barely covered things like water, soap, clothing-beyond the work jumpsuits, messaging time, internet time. There were many suicides, especially amongst the homeless workers.

The conditions at the factory were no different than the conditions that so called third world laborers around the globe suffered. There were no unions. The work could be dangerous and grueling, mundane, repetitive, thoughtless yet very important. Americans were hard workers. The world used to think of them as lazy and obese, but in the debt camps many worked the maximum, seventeen hours. People did not want to spend their lives working at the debt camps, so they pushed. They slept in the dorms. Those people suffered burn out, work related injuries and psychological issues.

Noel was staring at Samia from across the expansive factory floor. That day, going down the conveyor belt in front of Noel and the long row of standing workers were open PMDs that needed to be assembled. They had to connect wires and insert nanobot chips into the mechanisms. They did it over and over again. Noel knew the rhythm and could do ten personal messaging devices without thinking about it, without even looking sometimes. When the security guard from his sector stepped away to gossip with some other guards Noel quickly went over to Samia's workstation. A very low murmur started amongst the other workers, not with their mouths but with the rustling of clothing as they turned around to see what Noel was doing.

"Sam, are you alright?" He whispered as he knelt down and untied his shoelaces. He looked side to side nervously. She looked stressed but not injured.

"Yeah, Noel, I'm alright." Samia gave Noel a nod. Noel popped up, "OK good." He hurried back to his work station, relived that they had not hurt her.

The day's work was finally done and it was past midnight. The streets were completely dark, because it was lights off all over the city at exactly 12:00. Usually they might sleep in the dorms, but Samia wanted nothing to do with them. The still ripe waning moon, their headlights and other vehicle's headlights were all that illuminated the dark streets. The weary cousins didn't say anything to each other on the way home. They parked their hovees in a rickety little storage shed behind the house they shared with Samia's mom. Noel was her sister's son. She passed away when Noel was still a baby.

In their neighborhood there were many vacant, falling down houses. The population was still high with up to ten people living in some homes. The area had flooded several times, though the harbor was miles away. Some took it as a sign to move inland, others remained, determined to keep their homes. Gang on gang violence proliferated. Thunder fought Chaos constantly, killing many innocents. They heard a gun battle begin as soon as they got in the house.

Samia's mom Robin was already asleep when they got in. She had prepared MRE's for them to eat. It was a dish of dried chicken reconstituted into a soup, with a ball of rice and split peas. There were herbs and vegetables she grew in her illegal garden. Solar LED lights illuminated the kitchen. Samia grabbed her ready meal and ate it in her dark bedroom. She didn't want to talk and Noel didn't push her. She ate only to stop the hunger, she didn't taste anything. Later that night Samia laid in bed thinking about freedom and what it would be like to wake up and do what she wanted. She could go to school or ride her hovee anywhere she wanted to go. Their neighborhood was not quiet. The police sirens wailed constantly. She heard the rapid fire of a machine gun to the west. It was startling but too far to be of concern. That night was especially busy. Samia was so tired she was able to sleep through all of it.

The next morning Robin got ready for work. Breakfast consisted of some tough corn patties which were part of the food ration packets that everyone received per week. The garden gave them fresh peaches. She grew a plethora of vegetable. She grew herbs both for medicine and seasoning. She had a peach tree and an apple tree, but, the melons, strawberries for some reason never sprouted.

Samia's mom was a nurse. Because she was a health-care worker her personal debt and her family debt were lessened. People who worked in healthcare were allowed to work in their field to pay off their debt. No debt camps for doctors, dentist or surgeons. Samia had tried online health-care courses, but the bloody descriptions and then seeing the pictures of organs and veins, it made her literally sick. Noel tested low and could not become a health-care worker. He could clean the hospital, but his debt would remain the same. Robin heard Noel and Samia moving around in their rooms getting prepared for their day. Samia had been so close to freedom. Noel came out of his room first.

"Good morning Titi Robin," he said, calling her by the childhood name he had given her. He looked so much like his mother, the sister Robin lost.

"Good morning, Noel."

Robin's sister died with the many that were washed out to sea during the floods. Even though Robin was a single mother she took responsibility for young Noel when he had no one. Samia finally came out of her bedroom looking haggard.

"What happened to you all last night? Why did you come in so late?" Noel and Samia exchanged looks. Samia stuffed a piece of patty into her mouth and shook her

"Someone had a fight with a PID," Noel said looking at Samia. Her mother didn't know which one to look at.

"No Sam, tell me that Noel is lying."

"I did! They just got so nasty with me and I snapped."

"My dear, you cannot be carried by your anger into the

moments of your life. You must remain calm. You can't let the anger take over."

"Too late," Noel said quietly. Because they were monitored they sometimes wrote the things that could not be said. Robin wrote on a raggedy note pad, "U no how they get." Samia wrote, "I no. cannot help it so mad." They wrote small because after the paper was written on they ate or burned the pieces because all household trash was weighed and rifled through. Out loud Robin asked, "What happened to the PID?"

"I hit it."

"Nah, she didn't just hit it. She smacked it across the room. It was a rocket aimed directly at the head of the security guard who teased her about her period." Robin looked at her daughter with only slight disbelief. Samia always had a temper, but usually her rational side stepped in, that side seemed silenced. Noel continued, "She smashed it like it was a handball and dude was a great big wall. I think she got so much time because of that."

"Time?" Robin squinted at her daughter.

"I don't have to pay them back. They gave me six more

months."

"Six months on top of the years they already gave you?"

"Yep," Samia said dully and stuffed her mouth with the rest of her breakfast. She couldn't listen to her mother anymore. She didn't know how she would do another day working at the debt camp.

"We have to go. If I'm late I have to stay in the dorms tonight."

Robin got some paper to write on. She wrote a question down. Samia and Noel put on their boots and grabbed their bags.

"What r u going 2 do?" Robin wrote in tiny print.

She handed Samia the note and gulped because she had a feeling she knew what the answer was going to be. Samia took the pen from her mom and wrote under Robin's neat print.

"Providence." She handed her mother the paper and kissed her forehead.

"Bye mom." "Bye, Titi Robin."

Weeks after the PID incident the guards were still

harassing Samia daily. Some days it was milder than others. At any moment during her day Samia could be taken from her workstation and frisked, made to open her locker and bag for them to rifle through. They made her paint her boots over in front of them. Her check-ins involved thorough pat downs, sometimes semi-strip searches and daily walks through a metal detector.

One afternoon, things got worse. Samia was trying to get into the bathroom and two female guards were talking in front of the restroom door. The one with a large mole on her nose pushed Samia against the wall and searched her. She pulled out and stole the two dollars Samia had.

"Give me back my money, stupid idiot!" Samia yelled. It took everything Samia had not to hit the woman.

"Turn around, slave!" The other security guard said and mushed Samia's face into the wall. She tried to shield her teeth from hitting the wall by putting her lips over them. The guard kicked Samia's legs open and searched her too. The guard asked her if she had any alcohol, drugs or explosives. Samia struggled and was able to move her hand. She grabbed a chunk of the security guard's belly flesh and twisted digging her nails deep. The guard yelped and leaped back. Workers gathered, and though no one outright yelled at the guards, the worker's grumblings and unhappy murmurings were the only noises of outrage they could make safely.

The other guard grabbed Samia's arm. Samia told the guard that her mole looked like a mouse had taken a dump on her face. The smaller guard got her from behind and punched her in the kidney. Samia screamed and fell to the ground in pain.

Noel heard the commotion that had stopped all production. He hoped it was not Samia, but he knew. He was already running toward where she was when someone came to tell him that it was indeed his cousin getting her ass kicked.

As he was rushing to her, he saw some guards out of his peripheral vision and refused to stop. He heard Samia scream, and he knew he had to help her. He ran faster. One guard tackled him around his waist. He was able to shake dude off and run, but another rammed into him, and he fell down and his head hit a table. The guy was on top of him; he yelled and tried to push the guy off him, but then more guards came and were holding his legs. Three more guards came and he knew it was over for him. Samia was given more time on her debt. She got a text that warned her of prison if there was another serious offense.

That night they were still bruised up. They prepared dinner for Robin. When she got home she did not tell them about her drama filled day, with malaria cases on the rise, cholera outbreak victims who had to be quarantined and hydrated. Numerous dead and almost dead gang members shot in close range by military type weapons.

"Hey Noel."

"Hey Samia. How you all feeling?" She asked. She couldn't see the bruises that caused Samia to wince. Robin knew things at the factory had gotten terrible for Samia. She was confronted daily, bullied and provoked by the guards. Noel looked distraught.

Samia frowned and shook her head. On a piece of paper that already had scribbles from a conversation she had with Noel, Samia wrote, "I CANT DO DIS!"

Noel said, "Today was the worse we ever dealt with." Robin looked closely at her child. "Mom, they really messed me up today." Samia sagged and her mom hugged her. Robin felt her shaking. "There was a fight. They came at me, attacking me while I was trying to get into the ladies room," She said quietly into her mother's shoulder.

"I tried to get to her, but they jumped me, tackled me, hit me, anything to get me to stay. I've never seen them this out of control. There was nothing holding them back. No one seemed to have sense."

Robin rocked Samia like she was a little child needing soothing, "It's gonna be alright darling," she whispered. She let Samia go and she wiped her tears. Robin picked up some paper and wrote down something she had known for over a week, but didn't know how to tell Samia. She didn't want to let Samia go. She wrote it down as tears blurred her vision.

She wrote, "A boat at the harbor in 3 nites! 2 Providence!!"

She handed the paper to Samia almost shyly. Samia read the note and gasped. Juicy tears welled up and slid down her cheeks. She fell into her mother's arms and Robin held her up. Samia's legs were weak and her heart was racing. Noel took the paper and read it in disbelief. Burning tears filled his eyes threatening to fall. He didn't feel happy. He felt fear, disbelief and sorrow. Mother and daughter held each other feeling a mix of emotions. Samia felt dizzy and relieved. She cried and cried.

Noel wrote on the paper, "REALLY? HOW?"

Robin took some time to write, "At work. Patient talking 2 his family. Was in a hovee accident and has to have surgery. Tells his family he had to get on that boat. He didn't know when another boat going to Providence would come to Baltimore. After his family leaves, I ask him about it. At first he doesn't say anything. He lies. I give him a little more pain medicine to loosen his tongue. And he tells me everything."

Samia quickly read over Noel's shoulder. She stared at her mother in shock. Her mom was the most honest woman. It took some effort for Noel to read the note.

"Can it be it true?" Noel asked.

"I think it is, he had no reason to lie," Robin said seriously. Samia was glowing. She smiled as she tore the paper, popped it in her mouth and then took a sip of water as she chewed it up. The next few days they ate a breakfast of papers as they tried to work out how it was going to happen.

They agreed Samia would leave straight after work and Noel would ride with her most of the way there.

The morning she was leaving Samia hugged her mother somberly. They knew it could be the last time they saw each other. They wrote long notes to each other. Robin was tearful knowing her daughter might not make it. And once she got on the ocean, those waves, the flooding, the constant tsunamis...how would she navigate?

"I love you so much!" Robin said to her daughter.

"I love you too mom!"

Robin went into her purse and pulled out an envelope filled with cash. "This is to help you start your new life," she wrote. The lump in Samia throat made it hard to speak. She held her mother's hand till Noel said they had to go. She didn't want to let go of her mother.

"Bye Mom!" She yelled as she got on her hovee. She wanted to jump off and run to her mother, but she just sat there with tears and snot running down her face. Her heart was breaking. Her mother waved a weak hand at Samia.

Robin wondered if she made a mistake. Could it all end

tragically? She felt hurt and happy for her child at the same time. She kept waving good bye even after they rode away. Her tears made it hard for her to see. Robin went inside the house and prepared for work. She prepared for life without her child.

Walking in the quiet, abandoned neighborhood for the last time Samia realized how much she would miss her mom and Noel. Noel asked, "Are you sure about this?" They would work late and then leave for the Harbor after work. The boat was due on the west pier at 1A.M.

"If I stayed here...I don't know what would happen, but it wouldn't be good."

"Yeah, but at least you got family here." Noel felt sad and confused which came off as asshole.

"I want you to find freedom, but at what price? If the police stop us on the way to the Harbor, we will be in trouble. If we get caught by gangs...trouble. If we get caught by the water wall we go to jail."

"Noel I have to do this. I think if it was my debt...it's not even my debt."

"I know, Sam....it's just rough...I don't know about

this..."

"What do you mean?" Samia's heart and head couldn't hold anymore.

"What if it's a trap? What if it's not true and there is no boat?"

"I just have to take that chance." She put her hand on her cousin's shoulder, "Noel, I appreciate you being there for me all these years. You treated me like a sister and I'll never forget that." She started crying and hugged her cousin. Noel wanted to tell her not to do it. He didn't want her to go. He didn't say anything about that and hugged her back.

"I'm gonna miss you, Cuz." His throat felt dry and his eyes wet. They planned their trip through downtown Old Baltimore. Samia and Noel would separate once they got to the Harbor, she would have to get passed the water wall and security by herself.

It was a thirty minutes before midnight when they left the debt camp. They would still have streetlights for half an hour. The workday sucked and Samia got harassed by security, but no fights and they didn't do a random check of her purse or locker. If they did they would have found some suspicious stuff; ready meals, water disinfection tablets and lots of cash.

When they got on the road they took main streets where there would be streetlights. They didn't see any cops on the street. They got to an intersection on North Avenue, a few old school gas cars and hovees were on the street. Most of the stores and row houses were abandoned and badly damaged.

Samia gasped as hundreds of rats streamed out of the sewer. She had a severe case of the willies. There were rats in lines rushing, rats running into an old store. She had a panicked claustrophobic feeling. She was breathing shallowly into her helmet. The rodents ignored them. The ground was a moving thing, carpeted with them and they barely made room for them to ride through. Samia couldn't look down, she felt sick. Noel honked and shouted at them and they scattered. Samia was scared she would fall down into them. They could probably carry her away on their backs down into the sewer with them. With relief, the river of rats thinned out. The wind smelled foul, the sky ahead of them had a strange green glow. Samia reassured herself out loud that it was going to be okay. The cousins didn't stop to talk about it and just moved forward. They rode to a very brightly lit block and though they were relieved that there were no rats. Noel and Samia just wanted to get passed "D Block" as it was known. Somehow power stayed on in that area 24 hours a day. Noel stayed as close to Samia as possible. They rode quickly through the busy streets. It was noisy; cars honked, men laughed loudly, music blared out of strip joints. It was an overall circus type of atmosphere, but nothing was joyful under the spotlights. There were slaves, prostitutes, human trafficking and all types of sexual fast food to satisfy the unhealthy.

No one even saw or cared about the two young people on their hovees. There were others also on their hovees looking for something to do, and D Block did not disappoint, yet there were few cops around.

Samia was scared, but she couldn't turn back. She would not stop. She was glad to have her cousin with her.
It was a short block and after turning a corner they were quickly maneuvering down quiet abandoned looking streets. They headed down a street and heard dogs barking, owls, crickets. There were no streetlights and she knew it was after

midnight. The salty smell of the ocean permeated the air. They saw hovee headlights coming right towards them, the bright headlights were almost blinding. The people had portable spotlights too. They could not see and had to pull over.

"Keep your helmet on!" Noel told her. They stayed on their hovees as the other hovees rode closer. Noel only had a small knife to protect them. He counted three pairs of lights. Samia was freaking out. She was sweating and shaking. The hovees came up to them.

"What do you all want here?" A deep male voice said.

"We are just heading through. We weren't going to stop," Noel said. He sounded confident, though he was not at all. They shined their lights in his helmet. He didn't back up or take it off, but inside he was screaming, cursing scared as shit. Samia was so scared she struggled just to catch her breath. She knew she might have to speak too.

"But where y'all headed?" A voice with a very southern accent asked. Samia could not see any of them behind their bright lights. She felt exposed.

"You all are on private property," an angry sounding

female voice spat.

"We thought we were on the street, we didn't know this was private property," Noel tried to sound peaceful and calm. "Yes, this is a gated community and you are trespassing," the woman said. "We should report them, there's no place up there but the Harbor," she said to the others with her.

"Why are you all going to the Harbor?" They pointed their lights directly at her.

"I'm doing some research for my history class at school," Samia said. What she said was so stupid, she knew they were even more suspicious.

"You know you can get arrested for being over there."

"You know you can drown if the tide is in. A huge wave could cover you all up," said the voice with the accent.

"We won't get that close. The darkness caught us unawares, but we have gotten this far. We have just seen it online but never been there and wanted to experience what it was like."

"You all think we stupid, just git your asses out of here! Git, git! We calling the cops now!"
Totally shaken Noel and Samia quickly started their hovees

and sped away with the three on their tails. They were frantic, but they knew how to ride. All that playing they did on their hovees in the alleys behind their homes paid off. They out rode the neighborhood protectors who pursued them while screaming at the cousins. Samia felt something hard bounce off of her helmet. As they jetted out of that neighborhood those lights stayed shining on their backs till they were just pinpoints.

Samia cussed up a storm with relief and fear. She screamed. As they made their way down the once busy city streets near the Harbor Samia talked to herself.

"I cannot believe this! This shit is so crazy!" She couldn't believe all the obstacles. Around them were what used to be restaurants, coffee shops and pharmacies, they were all moldy, abandoned and wilted.

They got to the Harbor and Noel slowed down behind a broken up bus shelter. The water wall stood ahead of them huge and imposing like a mountain. It protected the city from the constant terrible floods.

Noel signaled for her to pull over. Samia pulled over and took off her helmet. She got off her hovee and jumped up and down, stomping her feet.

"Oh my goodness! Oh my freaking goodness!"

"I know that was so crazy!"

"Dang! I mean every time I tried to catch my breath it was something else." Noel got serious quickly, "Sam you have to go. Those people probably did call the cops. Keep your lights off. Use your PMD for lights. Your headlights are going to draw attention. I would say keep the hovee on low. You might have to ditch it. There's an entry with stairs somewhere that way."

Samia gave him a quick hug.

"Stay low. If cops stop you, act dumb."

"OK. Farewell Noel."

"Bye Samia." He did not get on his hovee. He watched her sadly. He looked around the empty streets and saw nothing but darkness. He knew the cops might be on their way at any minute. Samia started her hovee. It was so loud. She only had a few minutes to get to the boat. She waved at her cousin and rode towards the massive wall. The sound of her hovee echoed through the Harbor. It was deserted like the rest of the city. There were tall, empty skyscrapers with water lines that went up six stories.

Samia felt lonely. She was so scared, as she got closer to the wall she felt sicker. She wondered how she would get to what was behind the wall. She heard sirens. She cursed to herself knowing that they were looking for them. She wondered where Noel was. She was slightly panicked as she rode slowly and parallel to the water wall with her hand on it, she ran her fingers over the rough surface searching for a dip, an entry way. She saw the blue and red lights coming. Her stomach was in knots. She didn't know what to do. Suddenly, there was a large boom and Samia screamed. She saw a large fireball flare up into the sky. The ground rocked beneath her. She screamed again thinking about Noel and heard her own voice echo, echo, echoing down the street.

"Noel, what did you do?" Samia cried. Her legs felt weak. She fretted unable to proceed. She wanted to go find out if her cousin was alright. She was crying and hyperventilating in the darkness. The sirens were not approaching her anymore. She saw their lights going towards the explosion. The boom had bought her more time. The darkness weighed on her and things seemed to flash at her. There were invisible hands trying to get her, keep her locked in debt. She decided to ride her hovee back the way she had come and she ditched it behind the bus shelter where she and Noel had planned. She slung her bag over her shoulder and proceeded, using only her PMD as her light source. She ran carefully over the slimy, broken brick ground back to the looming water wall. She got to the wall and used her phone to see if there were any steps or doors, some way in. The wall was concrete gray with graffiti written all over it. The wall stretched into infinity on all sides of her. She was looking for some steps, a ladder, anything to get over.

She heard the sirens again and ran quickly along the wall. The sirens were closer and she could see their lights. Her heart sank. She was desperate. Her mouth was so dry. She just held her breath since she couldn't really breathe anyway. Finally, she saw what she was looking for; it was a dip in the wall. It wasn't big at all; it was a thin, little cut-out space that went all the way to the top of the wall. Samia shone her light over the length of it and saw something glinting. She stuck her hand in and felt something hard, cold and metal. She jiggled it and heard the clanging of what sounded like chains against something. She pulled and the thing came, she pulled harder, and the tall, metal ladder was almost out. She grunted using all her strength to pull out the rest of it. She shook the ladder and it was wobbly, when she started to climb it was very shaky. She got off the ladder and pulled it out some more. She strained to push it against the wall and something clicked. There was a strange whistle when she inhaled. She scampered up the ladder, this time it was less shaky. When she was half way up the metal ladder she heard the police sirens louder and louder. She rushed up and was almost to the top when she heard vehicles quickly approaching. She saw the headlights of a hovee zoom by followed by two regular cop cars.

"Go Noel!!!" Samia screamed. She was elated and petrified. She knew it was Noel. She was right. Noel gave them chase that entire night and eventually got away after hiding in an abandoned house for hours. He was the one that caused the explosions in one of the old school restaurants. Samia scrambled to the top of the ladder and had to heave her leg over the other side, thank goodness there was a ledge there. If she had turned on her light she would have seen there was a long way to fall down. She could hear the water gently hitting the pier. It was so quiet except for the police car sirens.

They zoomed past her again.

There was another ladder going down the wall. She slowly, carefully made her way down to the pier. She hummed quietly to tamp down her fear. She felt so much relief when her feet hit the ground. She stared gratefully at the black water that quietly lapped at the pier. She didn't know where to wait. She looked around nervously and took out her PMD.

It was a few minutes past 1 A.M!

Had she missed it, she wondered. She should have heard a ship as she was coming up the steps, or at least seen it leaving. She paced near the water looking ahead. She saw so many stars. She looked up at the stars and tried to remember the constellations her mother had taught her. She spotted Orion, the little dipper and the big dipper. She remembered her mom saying that the escaped slaves used the drinking gourd or the big dipper as their compass to freedom. Samia heard a strange hum. The water seemed to be bubbling and moving. She almost freaked out because there was nothing on the water and yet it was alive. The bubbles were large and a whirlpool developed on the water's surface. Then there was a strange light under the water. Samia's mouth was hanging open. Her eyes were wide and startled in the darkness.

A submarine slowly emerged and then the entire vessel was floating on the surface of the water. It had spotlights and headlights that were bright and they scanned the pier. Samia stood in the spotlight unable to move, covering her face and crying. The submarine went to the edge of the water. Samia looked up when she heard a strange grinding sound, some computerized beeping and then a door on the top of the submarine slowly opened up.

A tall black woman with long dreadlocks named Rose stepped out of the submarine and on the vessel and waved. Samia ran tearfully to the edge of the pier and touched the submarine. "We are on our way to freedom," the woman said as she gave Samia a hand up onto the vessel.

"Providence," Samia said looking at the woman and the submarine she was standing on in total disbelief.

"Providence." The woman repeated. "Come aboard then and meet your destiny!"

momentary
fulcrums

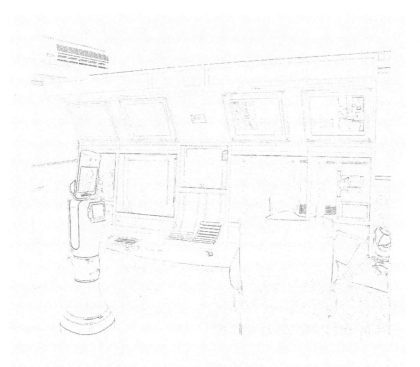

THE REVIVAL

BY RAVEN EKUNDAYO

Time changes and people evolve, but I get the feeling not everyone likes that. My dad was 22 in 2012 and he tells me stories about how everyone assumed things would be so different by now, about how technology would've advanced greatly and how relationships between races, cultures, etc, would've become more peaceful....

My dad is an optimist, always has been, but at 17 years old, I know better. I've read up on history and from what I can see things seem to always go around in cycles, but progression is balanced only according to whom you're asking. As I prepare to start my first year of college, I look at the world and I wonder how we got to this point. On one hand, there's "progress", but on the other hand, we're just as bad off as we were back in the Stone Ages, aka 1940. My dad had such high hopes for this country and this world, and in some instances, he's received the things he's prayed for. I just don't think he was prepared for the things that would come along with it.

Four, years ago we elected our first president of the same-gender-loving community. Alexis Vanderhyde comes from old money and had been married to her wife for 10 years. Eight years before becoming president, she joined the Senate; two years after that, she lead the charge to help pass a federal law making marriage equality legal in every state in the United States of America. For many, this was a day to celebrate; for others, this was another sign of the world ending. To be honest, I didn't really care at the time. At 17 years old, I can honestly admit political and religious issues like this didn't stare me dead in my face until about 2 years ago, when I had no choice.

After the federal law was passed, everyone assumed that people would magically begin to love and respect each other, but I've read my history books. I'm only a few generations removed from slavery, so I'm not sure why anyone thought in 2018, suddenly everyone would love gay people when so many still don't love Blacks, Jews, etc.

Every year following the ruling, there were horrible murders taking place all across the country, but they weren't geared toward the LGBT community; they were geared toward all minorities. They were random and brutal, and my dad told me that he assumed everyone would come together to battle a common foe, dad still being an optimist. Sadly, it only made matters worse between races because they all started blaming each other.

In 2026, at 15 years old, I was witness to the first televised execution. On October 23rd, 2026 a group simply named Revival sent a horrifying message to the entire world. At the time of the airing, Revival was known simply as a radical group made up of people from several different religious groups: Buddhist, Muslim, Hindu, Scientology, but the leader, whose name nobody knows to this day, was boldly

Christian. They stated that while they didn't agree on most things, they did agree that our society needed a clean slate. They believed that for too long we've allowed our ignorance and disrespect of faith to control our every move and that they were sent to set things right. My dad and I were confused because we didn't get why this made sense to any of them. At 15 years old, I felt like I was inside some crazy movie.

On the night of October 23rd, 2026, I was watching this concert on my Google iPad when it was interrupted by a man dressed like what society has come to know as "Jesus", meaning a white man with long brown hair and a beard. Even this version of Jesus he wore the sandals; but the rest of his outfit was different. He wore a tailored suit that looked like it cost a lot of money. He stood in what looked to be an office, but it was only half lit, you couldn't see behind him and his group. Everyone else within the group wore something that helped you distinguish their religion but they didn't go as far as their leader. All of them were dressed as if they were heading to a huge corporate affair. The Christian man began to speak. I ran downstairs to tell my dad. When I got to the living room I stopped in my tracks as I saw him sitting on the couch, mouth hanging open in disbelief. These Phalanx (a slang that means fools) found a way to take over every network. My dad tried every channel and there they were. The "Jesus" dude went on to explain that The Revival had come to realize that their threats were going unnoticed, and that they warned everyone that actions would be taken if everyone didn't start living their lives right. They stated that there would be consequences.

I spoke into the air, "Johnathan," and my best friend responded, "Dude, do you see this?" I was happy that this crap wasn't messing with the halo links we'd only purchased 4 days ago. Halo Links make it so you don't have to use text or call or anything like that with someone. You just set up the software in your house and provide it with your social and the names of anyone you want to connect with (First and Last name) and you can just speak into the air and it'll connect them wherever you are. If you're home no headset is needed but in public you wear something that resembles a blue tooth.

Anyway, I go on to ask him what does he think is about to happen. He said, "I don't know dude, but these motherfuckers are nuts." I giggled because my dad HATES cursing, but he paid no attention to what Johnathan said.

That alone let me know how serious this was to him. I don't think it grasped me that deeply yet.

"Jesus" said, "Two years ago, you chose to elect a sick beast as the leader of the free world. Since that time, you've continued to spit in the face of God. Before that, you passed a law letting these beasts marry, and this is all while still committing every sin under the sun. Abortion is STILL legal; most of you are having sex outside of marriage! You sicken me. My Buddhist brother is saddened because none of you know peace. None of you understand how to properly find enlightenment. My Muslim brother tires of feeling like this country only fears them, offers no respect or sadness for all the crimes committed against his people after 9/11. He tires of this country's ignorance." I noticed while watching this, none of the people in The Revival were women....

"Jesus" continued speaking. "Because you all have chosen to not listen to us and ignore our pleas to set your life on the right path, we must do God's will. For while we may differ on many things, we do agree that no matter what we may call our higher power, it is that higher power that rules us all, and you people have sadly forgotten that."

With that last comment, the Hindu brother flipped the switch, and you could see a conference table. Around the conference table were 10 people with hoods over their faces. Each member of The Revival went around the table removing the masks and you could see that all of them had been gagged as well. They saved one person for last and left their hood on.

Each person appeared to be some totally random person. A white woman who looked to be in her late 30's, an Asian man who looked to be in his 50's (from what I could tell from his face, may have been blind, a Black man who looked to be in his late 20's, who honestly looked far too strong to have been captured by these people. They all had looks of total horror on their faces. "Jesus" spoke, "You see what needs to happen is there needs to be an apology made to my Lord and Savior. You all have sinned within an inch of your life, but you see, He loves you anyway. I've decided tonight that I will do my best to follow his will and forgive you two. I will forgive all of you by showing you what true sacrifice is. Once you understand true sacrifice, The Revival will wash its hands of you and continue to do our work to better this great nation."

"Jesus" then removed the hood off the final person and my dad gasped. Johnathan and I were lost. I said to my dad, "Who is that?" to which he replied, "Braxton Strauss, Secretary of State." At the time, I can admit I had NO clue what that meant (I do now though). He didn't see the look on my face, as he couldn't turn his face from the TV. All I could wonder was if this dude was kidnapped, where was the President, and was she okay.

"Jesus" spoke, "Mrs. Vanderhyde, it looks as though you're so concerned with keeping security around you, your "Life Partner", and those abominations that you call children that you totally left the rest of your cabinet wide open. I honestly wanted your Vice President to be sitting here and not Mr. Strauss, however; it looks as though someone was smart enough to be out of the country for an entire week. I wonder if he knew; I wonder if that sad excuse for a human being knew that we were coming for his traitorous soul. How dare he call himself a God-fearing Christian and support you or anything you stand for. Vice President Harmon is a coward that didn't have the balls to stick to anything he said when he ran against you and had the nerve to accept your request to be the VP of this wonderful, but weak country. When we find you Harmon..." His voice trailed off, and he looked like he was in a trance. His face was beat red and sweat was slowly coming down his forehead. A drop touched the tip of his nose and it was if it woke him up. He wiped his face and continued, "Get the knives...."

Johnathan said, "Dude, what are they about to do?"

"I have no idea..." and my voice trailed off. My dad stood up and looked away from the TV for the first time since it all started and headed upstairs, All I heard him say was "Diane" which is my aunt's name, my mom's sister, and she replied "My God Warren..." and he vanished into the bedroom.

I sat on the couch and Johnathan said, "Dude, what the fuck?" as we watched in shock as the Muslim brother brought out a bag filled with machetes. Each member of The Revival pulled out one machete and stood behind one of the 10 people. Because there were only 5 members of The Revival there were 5 people with no one behind them.

My knees became weak. I whispered to myself "I know this can't...they're not about to..."

Johnathan said, "Dude, this is insane, where the hell are the police, dude? Where are the fucking police?!"

"Jesus" spoke, "A sacrifice will wash away all of your sins. You all will learn to fear God and to respect his mighty power. *'But from everlasting to everlasting, the Lord's love is with those who fear him and his righteousness with their children's children', Psalms 103:17.* What we do today shall be passed down from generation to generation and we can only hope that your children will learn from your sins."

He became silent and raised his machete over the head of the 30-something white woman with his left hand; with his right hand he removed her gag. "Do you have anything you want to share with the world before you give your life to the Lord?" The woman screamed, "DEAR GOD! PLEASE LET ME GO! I HAVE 2 KIDS AND A HUSBAND!

He covered her mouth and said, "God will let you go, my sister. *'For what the law was powerless to do because it was weakened by the sinful nature, God did by sending his own Son in the likeness of sinful humanity to be a sin offering. And so he condemned sin in human flesh.* Romans 8:3.'"
With that he took the machete to her neck...

DREAM CATCHER

BY FERNANDO QUIJANO III

My eyes open at six. I sit up, touch my pad on, and begin
reviewing my dreams. I don't remember them. I never do. I
know why. They're boring. There are a few good ones—sex
dreams, dreams where I'm bouncing over trees and buildings,
dreams of flying. Those are few and far between.

I touch my keyboard up and type in some basic
descriptions—*shaving in a desert with sand and a rock, a ride
on a bus next to a stranger speaking gibberish, in a
laundromat waiting for a dryer.* Mundane things. A waste of
time.

A beautiful girl. I hope this is a sex dream. *She stares at me. She says, "Be free," and walks away.* I want to follow her. I can't. I have to go to work. I touch some music on—top forty—and head for the shower.

"One last thing," says the man at the front the crowded room, "I was sorry to hear that Macy's has finally filed for Chapter Seven."

The room breaks out in a loud, sarcastic *awwww.*

"I know," says the man, "we're all heartbroken."

Someone raises a hand.

"Yes!"

"Are we buying them out?"

"Excellent question. We made them an offer last year. They turned us down, but I'm sure we can snap up some of their inventory as they liquidate. Anyway, that's enough gloating, for now—at least until The Wal goes under. This is inventory weekend. We have a lot of ground to cover, as usual. Let's make sure we keep everything in order. Nobody wants to count all this shit, as is. Let's not make our job harder.

"Redshirts, move out. Somnian, if I could just speak to you for a moment."

I make my way to the front as everyone else filters back to the sales floor. "You asked to see me?"

"Yeah. We got a report this morning from Tech. They need you to go in for a scan, maybe some maintenance."

"Sure," I reply, "I'm off tomorrow."

"They want to see you, today," he says, "It's probably nothing, but you know how it is. If something goes wrong, it can go *really* wrong. They've gotten approval to let you use some personal time. Rolley's going to cover your shift. You can leave now."

The ride to Tech is always fascinating. I live walking distance from the job, so I don't get to take the Red Line very often, except when I'm headed to the harbor. Shit at the Inner Harbor's too pricey for someone like me. The only time I go is when I have company from out of town. Truth is, my friends can't afford it either.

I pick it up right outside the Mall. Everything starts off barren as the train passes through the commuter corridor that connects the city to its western suburbs—Medicare, Medicaid, Social Security, and the mall, of course. We drop into a tunnel at the city line and pop back up a couple of minutes later in Edmondson Village. This part of the city begins like a suburb, with its lovely little houses and their lovely little driveways. Any sense of loveliness fades as we pass Edmondson Village Shopping Center.

Lovely houses give way to blocks of cramped rowhouses, many of them boarded up. Security is thick at Allendale Station—men in riot gear spread out on the platform, batons firmly in hand. The same is true as we pass through Rosemont and the MARC station. The Red Line has only been in operation for seven years, and they've already shut down the stations in Harlem Park and Poppleton. Anyplace you need to get to between the MARC and Howard Street means a long walk, not that anyone in their right mind —anyone not already living there, if you can call it living— would walk into the Red Zone. Even I wouldn't be that stupid, and I grew up in the Red Zone.

I graduated from Harlem Park Middle in 2012. Things were different. After years of decline, groups had come in to work with the kids—planting gardens, teaching music and art, treating us like we were normal people, filling us with hope, dreams. And then everything began to fall apart.

The decline was gradual, but it felt sudden. *No More Free Rides* was the slogan that spread like herpes starting in 2013. No one was a victim of poverty. We were culprits, complicit in our condition. We all wanted nothing more than to collect a government check, live in subsidized housing, and have babies that the government had to pay for.

By my junior year in high school, deficit reduction meant the free rides truly were over. Social programs that weren't cut were eliminated. The national wave of *Personal Responsibility* rolled over every poor, urban neighborhood hitting neighborhoods like Harlem Park harder than a Japanese tsunami.

The groups that had been working there tried to reinforce their efforts, but having lost their federal funding, there was not much they could do. As SNAP, what the old heads called Food Stamps, was phased out, soup kitchens and food pantries popped up all over to fill the void. Some voids are too big to fill. It wasn't long before the riots started.

Rioting happened all over the country. Baltimore wasn't unusual in that regard. But the West Baltimore riot during the summer of 2015 was memorable, nevertheless. I was one of the lucky ones. My high school, Baltimore Polytechnic, had been proactive, identifying which of their students had special needs, students whose parents had their benefits reduced, or had lost them, entirely. They managed, with the help of alumni, to get us jobs so that we could at least buy uniforms and supplies.

I was on my way home, walking from the restaurant in Hollins Market where I washed dishes. I was making my way past a food pantry. What had started as a few people yelling in the unbearable August heat as I approached turned into *everyone* screaming at the top of their lungs, the crowd pushing, surging towards the doors of the pantry, the volunteers trying their best to hold them back. They had run out of food. I paused for a bit across the street, curious to how this was going to play out. I left as trashcans and tree branches began to fly through the pantry windows. When I heard the gunfire—repetitive, unceasing gunfire, not the sporadic gunfire you hear when the slingers are fighting for territory—my heart began to beat its way through my chest, fast and hard.

By morning, as I made my way back to work, so much of the old neighborhood was nothing more than burnt out husks; and it wasn't over—not even close. Rioting went on for nights as the tired and desperate poor broke curfews to lash out against their own brothers and sisters, against the few businesses that had survived the government's austerity measures. Within a week, the Westside was a war zone with National Guard troops patrolling the very corners that the drug slingers once held.

When the school year started, my senior year, I was forced to carry I.D. to get in and out of the neighborhood. Much of the Westside had been fenced off. Everyone began to call it the West Bank. I didn't bother with college after graduation. I got a job with *Big Red* and found a place in Woodlawn where I could take care of my mother, where I could keep her safe.

Bayview is the next to last stop. I get off and head to the Tech building, the same place where I'd had my *Assistant* installed. Inside, the lady at the front desk greets me by name. "Welcome, Mr. Somnian," she says as she hands me a passcard, "You're expected upstairs in suite 331."

In 331, I'm reclining in a comfortable chair, the same type of chair I sat in as they installed my *Assistant*. The technician is on a stool on casters, rolling around me, tapping away on his pad. "Any problems with your waking protocol?"

"No. I'm awake at six every day, like clockwork."

"Looks fine," he says, "Let's talk about your dreams."

"My dreams? Why? I log them all."

"Absolutely." he says, excitedly. "I reckon you're one of the most diligent dream loggers I've met. This morning. You logged a dream about a woman?"

"Yeah, but I dream about women all the time. It makes up for not having one in my life."

"Right. Well, it's never too late."

"Have you seen my paycheck?"

He laughs at my lame joke. He goes on. "This woman, she mentioned something about being free."

"That's right. See for yourself. It should still be in the buffer."

The technician picks up my pad, taps on it a few times. He watches, taps, watches. Finally, I hear the voice. "Be free."

"Is there a problem?"

"I'm sure it's nothing. We've experienced a few glitches with some *Assistants*. All of them began with similar dreams. It's a good thing you're so thorough with your logs. It could have turned into a problem had you been neglectful. We're just going to put you under for a few, make some preventative adjustments to insure everything is shipshape. We wouldn't want you to miss any important calls, right."

"No sir," I say, sarcastically, "I wouldn't want to have any interruption to my social life."

"Good. I'm going to step out for a few, see another customer. A nurse will be in to administer the anesthesia. Just sit back and relax."

I do as he says, sinking deeper into my recliner as he exits. Within seconds, a young lady walks in dressed in scrubs. She's familiar, attractive—auburn hair pulled back in a neat bun, thick lips drenched in glossy pink, skin like *cafe au lait*—but I can't quite place her.

"Do I know you?" I ask, "I'm sorry. I know you must get that a lot. But you look *so* familiar."

"That's because I was in your dreams last night," she says, casually, as if it were no big deal.

"That ain't right," I say, smiling, "Isn't it unethical to fuck with someone like that, at least not if you're not dating."

She doesn't smile. She either doesn't get or doesn't appreciate my attempts at flirty humor.

"Listen to me," she says, seriously, "We don't have a lot of time. The tech will be back in ten minutes, maybe less. That doesn't give me much time to disconnect your *Assistant* —"

"What are you talking about? Why would you do that? How would I receive calls? How the fuck would I even get up in the morning?"

"Solomon, calm down," she says, "Trust me—"

"Trust you? Bitch, I don't even know you! How're gonna just use my name like that?"

"Please, Solomon. Just listen. I know you think things are wonderful. You have your job. You're mother's safe.

You're better off than plenty. But you need to be free."

"What are you talking about? I *am* free. Isn't that what you said in my dream? How did you do that, anyway? Why?"

"I have a better question," she says, "Why do people have to start logging their dreams when they have their *Assistants* installed?"

"What?"

"It's not a complicated question."

"The tech who installed it said something about interference... certain dreams can mess with the system... it could break down. He said a replacement would be more a lot more expensive than fixing the one I got."

"Right," she says, picking up where I trailed off, "because your original *assistant* was free, as long as you commit to a network."

"Right."

"So why are you here, now?"

"Because they caught one of those precursor dreams. Because they want to fix it before it gets worse."

"And you believe them? Because something so simple, so internal, like a dream can be powerful enough to compromise something so high tech."

"Who are—"

"That doesn't matter. Not now. We don't have the time for introductions. The reason they want you to log your dreams is because they knew that it would be a matter of time before someone would figure out how to broadcast right to your head. We've finally jumped that hurdle."

"Who's we?"

"Seriously, Solomon, shut up. It's not important, not yet. What's important is that you understand that we chose you. You grew up in the West Bank. You went to Poly. You have a unique understanding of life on both sides of the fence. We need you inside. We need people that understand that it's wrong to isolate and ignore a whole segment of society just to balance a budget so that those who have plenty can keep more of it; that it's wrong to turn neighborhoods into nothing more than feeders to keep prisons profitable and wages down."

"What do you expect me to do about it?"

"Solomon, are you happy?" she asks, casually, as if the conversation hadn't just been frighteningly serious.

"I'm fine."

"Lots of people are fine, Solomon. Are you happy?"

I can't bring myself to answer.

"It's okay. No one's happy. We've all just been sold a hardline to permanent contentment. We're given just enough to keep us from being miserable, just enough for us to forget those who are. You can end this. All you have to do is close your eyes and let me disconnect your GPS and take you offline. Or I can put you under, and when you wake up, you can go back to your life of... contentment, if that's what you want to call it. Decide now."

It is so much to process. "And then what?"

"Close your eyes, Solomon, and find out."

My eyes close.

CHANGE FOR A FIVE

BY JASON HARRIS

Cory stood at his normal perch in the Mertz Rental facility, adjacent to the airport, surveying the automated vehicles as they zigzagged through the parking lot, each following its programmed drive path and moving out towards their destinations. Some of the vehicles would pull over to the curb where newly arrived renters would jump into the cars, bags in hand, and speed off the lot.

To Cory, it reminded him of a tapestry in a museum, a multi-shaded palette of threads stitched and woven at a breakneck pace, breaking off, stopping and starting, the blur of curved forms punctuated by the squeal of tires on the pavement. He checked one of the monitors that wrapped around the desk in front of him to see what was scheduled. Data cascaded down the page that corresponded to the lines of cars in the lot. When the schedule wasn't so heavy, he could actually read and keep track of the data; but those days were few and far between. He rarely had any tasks to do, other than troubleshoot when a car didn't respond to its instructions and went off course. Last year, he only had 3 instances of these 'route permutations' as his co-worker Sunil liked to call them.

In the living room on his wall at home, Cory still proudly displayed the plaque he received at the holiday banquet for averting a disaster with the last of the accidents; that day, he had overrode the dispatch system to keep four rogue cars that were careening through the lot via altered paths from running into the rest of the fleet. "Car #42876r", he would say, using the inventory control number while recalling the number of each vehicle as he recounted his heroism. If he was at the bowling alley, he would be more to the point, "The first one was a silver Ford Focus 5-door. Windows were down and the stereo was even blasting." Cory had memorized the old keyboard shortcut to bring up the override screen, which was still present in the system despite that fact that it had been updated. Sunil had written a patch for the system that effectively fixed the glitch that produced the route permutations, leaving Cory to muster up enough professionalism to stand sentry over a fleet for which he could do nothing. He would muse to the screens in front of him, "It kinda feels like I'm riding in one of the cars all day, but I'm just standing here watching them go."

When Model 1 of Electronic Data Associates Automated Route Protocol Administration Units (ARPAU) arrived at the rental facility, Cory thought about how 12 years after he had finished at CCBC- Essex, today might be his last day of work. Ever. While he prided himself on his methodical approach to his job, he wondered how he was he gonna be able to compete with a *thing*. The ARPAU 1 was a sleek, rectangular box on wheels that was jacked directly into the monitoring console in the station. A telescopic pole with some type of camera device sat on top of the box, and from what Cory could discern, served as the eyes and ears of the unit. The engineer who was installing the robot with Sunil's assistance was less than forthcoming, which Cory took as a sure sign that the end was near for him. He tried humor: "Does it take smoke breaks?" The engineer didn't even bother to look up when he responded. "Not hardly, and I hope you don't smoke in here, because it has a built in smoke alarm system." Sunil was empathetic.

"Cory, don't worry, this is a pilot program, so we need you to help work out the bugs in this system."

"Thanks Sunil, but that's not exactly reassuring," Cory said as he stepped out to get some air.

Tammy passed by Cory in the parking lot, pushing her cart, laden with the brooms, towels, sprays and vacuums she used to clean the offices around the lot. She was never one to mince words, even when she was in one of her better moods.

"Looks like they trying to put you out with the trash, homey," she mused when she passed. She laughed, one of those hacking, hybrid cough chuckles that come out of folks when they are party or witness to something that has them questioning the what's and whys of their own existence.

"Much money as you saved this company, they 'finna replace you with a fancy X-box." Cory was too out of sorts to be angry about it.

"Nothing I can do, Tam. I've worked hard since the day I got here, and that's what I'm gonna do until they tell me my time is up."

"I hear what you saying Cory, I just think it's messed up. You a good dude and you always done your job well. No reason for them to put a robot in your spot." Cory shrugged, finished his soda, and went back to his station.

Six months, three motherboards, two power supplies and 5 data cables later, ARPAU 1 was re- moved from the station. A tight smirk was affixed on Cory's face as the same engineer, now humbled, quietly dismantled the bot and rolled it out of the station, without even apologizing for repeatedly accusing Cory of sabotaging the unit. Cory had shrugged when the camera unit was installed in the station three months into the project to monitor his interaction with the robot. "Interact?" he guffawed when discussing the initiative with Francella, his manager. "What interaction? This isn't one of those android units they show on wired.com; the thing doesn't talk, and the only reason it looks at me is to record video of me doing something so it can replace me!"

"It is not going to replace you, Cory. There will always be something for you to do here; but let's face it, you get paid to stand and look at traffic all day."

"I disagree, Fran; I get paid to make sure that these cars don't go off track and kill somebody. I think I am worth my salary just for that."

"You are worth it for that, Cory, but we haven't had a permutation since Sunil patched the system. So there isn't much for you to do." When the ARPAU 1 was removed, Francella brought Cory lunch. "Well, you outlasted R2D2." Now it was Cory's turn to laugh.

"Yeah, this round. I'm sure they'll be back."

ARPAU 3 arrived 14 months after ARPAU 1 had been removed. This unit still required being plugged into the wall, but the torso of the unit looked more like a human torso. The torso was placed on three legs with wheels for feet, along with an articulating arm. Atop the torso sat a square head on a swivel, with two circular lens protruding out the front of the head that served as ocular sensors and two grilled openings under the eyes, one for speaking and one for recording sound.

"Hello", the unit said in a choppy, digitized croak, head swiveling in Cory's direction.

"Well alright, I like this one already," Cory replied, "but it needs a little more hair on its head if it's gonna be as handsome as me."

The engineer, a different one this go round, smiled. "I'll go back to my car and see if I left the wig unit in there."

Cory felt upbeat but the improvements of this unit meant that he would soon be out of a job, no matter what fluff Francella tried to sell to him.

"Don't worry hon; this thing will probably be more of a bucket of bolts than the first unit." Tammy unwittingly made Francella out to be a prophet; 3 months in, ARPAU 3 trapped Tammy in the monitoring station when she passed through to vacuum the area after hours. The unit's security protocol was tripped off because it was programmed for human interaction based on Cory's work schedule. The unit blocked the door when Tammy attempted to exit and when she pushed the unit aside, it grabbed her arm with its own in an attempt to right itself, and severely dislocated the frightened janitor's shoulder along with fracturing her wrist. The engineer had removed the unit before Cory even arrived at work the next day.

Cory ventured downtown to walk the Inner Harbor one weekend when he saw Tammy; it was about 4 months after the accident, and she was out with her family. Her arm was still in a sling, probably because she was still waiting for a settlement check from the vendor; based on the nature of accident, Cory and his coworkers figured Tammy would be getting something in the low six figures. Tammy looked like she was already spending the money.

"Hey Cory! They replace the terminator yet?"

"Hey Tam, nope, it's just me right now. How are you feeling?"

Tammy laughed. "I'm feeling okay, but I'll feel a lot better when I get my check. Y'all," she said to her kids, "this is the man who work with that crazy robot in his office. Say hi to Mister Cory." The kids all mumbled some type of greeting, more interested in their cotton candy or a game on their Com than the man who worked with their mother. Cory in turn greeted them, all the while wondering if they would ever get an opportunity to work when they were older, or would this moment be a preview of both his and their future stations in life, just walking aimlessly all day, eating confections while machines ran the world.

When ARPAU 5 arrived, Cory and Tammy had gotten comfortable enough to think that there might not ever be a replacement. Cory had already received his letter of commendation for 15 years of service; Tammy's arm was completely healed and she was back, happy and bragging about the things she was able to do with the windfall gained from being "assaulted by that death-bot." ARPAU 5 quickly put things back into perspective. The first thing Cory noticed is that while it still had wheels, it wasn't plugged into the wall or the console. This unit definitely looked more robot than science project gone wild; the metal casing for the unit was burnished bronze and it featured two articulated arms and a head that was shaped like a human cranium. Its ocular sensors blinked and the unit's voice did not have the tinny, synthesized quality that humans were accustomed to hearing from anything artificial. ARPAU 5 spoke in measured tones that sounded like a voice one would hear on the radio.

"Good morning, Cory. I am your new assistant. My name is Five."

"Hi, Five." Cory cringed at the inadvertent pun.

"So you're my replacement, huh? Have they worked out all of your bugs?" The unit quietly clicked and computed a response.

"I am here to help optimize the flow of traffic for routes in the greater Baltimore Metro District."

ARPAU 5 blinked with an audible click as Cory walked out of the station and headed to Francella's office. "So this is it." Cory slumped in the chair across from his boss's desk.

"This model looks like the real thing, and talks like it graduated from Hopkins with high honors. How long do I have before I transfer to something else?" Francella was quiet. She was looking at her Com's monitor, but her attention was there merely as a diversion from addressing Cory.

"Fran, look, I don't want to find out on my last day that I'm gone. Can I get a transfer?"

Fran rubbed her temples and looked at Cory.

"I'm sorry Hon. I was able to get you two months."

"Okay that's cool, so in the meantime I train the bot and...," Francella interrupted Cory.

"No hon, I mean I was able to get you two months' severance. Those bastards wanted to give you two weeks. Today's your last day. 15 years, only 3 days sick and never late. Meanwhile we've gone through 3 of those bots in the last 4 years and none lasted more than 6 months. That was my argument to them, so that got you two months."

Cory spent the first two weeks of the rest of his life indoors. His rent was paid, and at worst, he could consolidate and move out of his meager one-bedroom into a rooming house, but beyond that he didn't know what he would do. He knew those screens, knew when things were going good, and for so long, knew how to fix things when they went bad. Now, he was worthless, and some geek's thesis project was standing in his station, doing his job. The thought of even seeing an automated car hurt him to his core. Francella had given him some leads, and Tammy gave him an application from her cleaning company, but the wound to his pride, his sense of accomplishment, was deep and required time to heal before he could move back out into the world. His buddies at the bowling alley were sympathetic as he ranted, "If anything beyond a normal route permutation occurred, that fleet and whoever is in its path is doomed because that bot is not going to know what to do. You can patch bugs, but you can't upload common sense."

Three weeks into what he termed his "career stoppage", Cory was back downtown, this time watching traffic; specifically the automated lane, which with the exception of the bike lanes, was closest to the curb. He could easily spot cars from his fleet mixed in with vehicles from competing rental companies and automated taxi services as they moved down the street, some stopping to take on or release passengers. According to Francella, Mertz was the only company that had gone with a fully automated system; other companies still had humans in the mix in regards to fleet and route management. No one outside of Cory seemed to care one way or the other. He was watching one of his cars, a white Chrysler sedan #61322L, as it was cut off by a van that pulled into the automated lane from the middle lane. As programmed, the sedan stopped; Cory was glad that at least the sensors on the car worked fine. Two men jumped out of the van and one held a black box that he pointed towards #61322L. The man then opened the back door of the sedan and ran back to the van, assisting the second man in carrying a large suitcase to the sedan. They pushed the suitcase into the back seat, and the second man slid into the seat with the bag and closed the back door. The first man jumped back into the van and quickly pulled back into traffic, almost hitting a cursing courier on his cycle.

Cory watched as the sedan recalibrated its path and began to move again, no doubt resuming its route. He began to run down the sidewalk next to the car. The man in the backseat was not looking at him; he seemed to be involved with the suitcase. Cory got a sick feeling in his stomach. Would he be able to see what had occurred on the permutation screen or the vehicle security breech list? He tried to calculate the delay. A minute and a half tops. What about the weight of the passenger and bag? It took two men to carry the bag to the car. That and the fact that they hacked the doors to unlock them had him reaching for his phone as he arrived at a crosswalk. The sedan turned onto Pratt Street headed towards the power plant and the World Trade Tower. Cory ran across the street and caught up to the car. He banged on the window, startling the man in the back. Their eyes briefly met, and Cory looked beyond him and saw that the suitcase was open, containing therein a grim looking device. Whatever it was, it was obviously turned on.

Francella said, "Hey" into his Com's ear-piece just as Cory saw a tear run down the man's face; a nanosecond later, sound and sight were replaced by a pure white light carried on the wing of a hot wind that pushed through Cory and everything within two square miles. Francella heard nothing but static yet even in her office 15 miles away, windows rattled. The ARPAU 5 was interfaced wirelessly and the blast broke its connection to the route system, but its ocular-audio unit could still monitor the data coming from #61322L. The permutation screen was going crazy, as every vehicle within the region was reading offline. ARPAU 5 reported this as a major system failure and began checking the transmission lines for breaks that would cause this many objects to register permutations. Meanwhile, a single thought, processed but not soon enough committed to speech, floated into the troposphere with the fallout from below, echoing the confident final statement of the first fallen as an ethereal epitaph: "A cab driver or I could have caught that."

PEDAGOGICS

BY JASON HARRIS

The road presented a challenge that neither the speed, type of vehicle, weather condition or skill of the individual traveling upon it mattered. Almost two decades of use without proper maintenance left a sculpted terrain more akin to path than avenue; yet here they were, long past nightfall, gingerly traversing it long after street lamps were blacked out. The only sound that could be heard, besides the strains of Parliament's "Knee Deep" wafting from the stereo, was the scrape and crackle of the tires rolling over the rough pavement. Downtown's light cast a glow in the sky that was enveloped by the stillness on this block; the headlights of the car screamed against the darkness, but in the end, even 10000 lumina could not outshine the shadows.

The GPS screen was set to pedestrian mode, and on the screen, random blips moved about on the periphery of the car's path. "People", said I said, pointing towards the screen. SamJack nodded in assent and remained mute.

"*Something about the music/ it got into my pants,*" cooed the voices in the song. The silence in relation to the apparent activity on the road made me antsy. Curfew laws meant I seldom ventured outside the west side, and while I recalled visiting this area when I was younger, I had not been back since it had "died" and became an empty municipality. SamJack had politicked hard with Titi to get permission for me to accompany him, driving all the way over to the east side to scoop me up from school.

Titi and SamJack went back and forth for what seemed like an hour before Titi relented.

"Titi," SamJack said, "the time that he spends working on the minutia that passes as school work is time taken away from his destiny! You know that as well as I do."

"Destiny?" Titi humphed. "When and where did your brief yourself on his destiny? Did you consult the Dagara wheel? Orunmila? The Metu Neter? Allah? You don't even grasp the significance of your own destiny, let alone his."

Titi's furrowed brow did not match the calm timbre of her voice. "And even if you do know his destiny, that doesn't mean he should be out running the streets with you Sam."

SamJack's glare bounced off of the back of Titi's head as she turned away disinterested walked out of the living room towards the kitchen. All the while I was riveted, because I had never seen anyone challenge Titi, and had certainly not seen SamJack speak to Titi as an adult instead of a Mother Elder. I felt like my cousin was fighting on his behalf, but that did not keep me from feeling nervous. I had heard enough in the school hallways and out on the block to regard SamJack as dangerous if the lore surrounding him was even half way accurate. I simply couldn't understand at this point why SamJack would go against Titi for me.

Titi sighed after she realized that both Sam and I had followed her into the kitchen. "Where do you plan on taking him?"

"Out to the county to a church meeting Tuesday evening."

"Okay, Sam,' suddenly Titi sounded like an old woman. She drew her finger across her neck; "I don't want him near any guns or mayhem; have him back by 11. It's a school night." SamJack smiled; a rarity. "Titi, this spot is chill, and you should know that rolling with me is the safest way he can travel in this city."

Titi huffed. I can remember her saying SamJack's heart was right handed, but he acted with his left hand, with his good intent often buried beneath the calamity of his actions. Titi had consulted Pomba Gira to see SamJack's destiny when he was young, and in the center of his life force firmly stood Ogum; master of War and Politics.

"You finally roll with me today," was all SamJack had said on Skype, hanging up before I could ply him for information. When he pulled up after school, I realized that I didn't even know that SamJack had a car- I had only seen him on a motorcycle or bicycle prior to today. "When did you get this car?" I could no longer stand the silence.

"Sedrick and I bought this like 2 years ago. He drives it more than I do," he replied. "I prefer riding my bikes, but

this spot here is no place for a bike, unless you rolling deep."
Now I was more nervous than before, "then why did you
want me to ride with you out here? What am I supposed to
be, your bodyguard?" SamJack had to laugh at that; "This is
a field trip for you, Dream. I was talking to Titi about you a
few days ago and she told me about the books you were
reading for the university program; that's why I came over
last night to see about you coming with me. I want you to see
what's going on outside those books of yours."

So I settled back, momentarily lost in thought. Was SamJack a
gangster? He couldn't be a drug dealer; anything that was
worth selling could be ordered from Amazon or picked up
from CVS, and the drugs that were illegal to possess and sell
were so dangerous, rarely did one live long enough to enjoy
the fruits of their labor. At this stage dealing drugs was a
scattershot hustle, which went against the calculated manner
in which SamJack always seemed to move. All of his
endeavors seemed to require subterfuge, and I struggled to
figure out what that meant. "Sam...are you selling?" I started
but I was at a loss of what to ask.

"Selling what, ice cream?" SamJack was laughing again.
"Dream, you've been watching too much of that old
video- nobody does any of that stupid shit they used to do 20
years ago. You'd be locked up before you could ask for a
lawyer, and that's if you weren't already dead."

"I am a freelancer. I make my money outside of the
normal channels of commerce. I don't have a regular job, I'm
my own boss, I work when I want, where I want, and I take
jobs based on how much money I want to make. We are
going to one of my regular gigs now."

"Look at it this way Dream; damn near everybody we know in the city works for Big Cuz, (CUHS - Consolidated University Hospital System). Think of a job, and a person working that job, and who is their boss? Big Cuz. The last straw for me was when I got in trouble for drag racing on I-70. You may not remember this because you were little. They sent me up for 3 months to the Sykesville Work camp and I had just turned 16. You know who owns that prison? Big Cuz. Anything that I did wrong meant a month was added to my work assignment. I was 17 when I was released- I had months added for stuff like not having my bed made, talking back to the work foreman, and fighting. The day I left I straight told the warden that I would never work for Big Cuz again."

"So in the classic sense," SamJack chuckled, "I was successfully rehabilitated, but in the political sense, I was enraged. Instead of assigning us to do the things that would help the city, our work was contracted out to corporations. As a work assignee, that meant no pay, and we were assigned to put together Vid Terminals, Furniture, and work in Big CUHS factories."

I was so immersed in listening to what SamJack was telling me, I was surprised when I looked up and realized that the barren urbanity had given way to a wider expanse with lights and an occasional car; I did however notice when SamJack set the cruise controller on the car to 70 km, as outside the border, the speed cameras became cruisers, peopled by those eager to arrest, impound and plunder.

"You are being put on a track to work for Big CUHS because of your talents. As far as I'm concerned, that is a problem. Your intellect and creativity should not be put in the service of something that allows people to starve blocks away from where they have enough food to feed the city and not even be close to running out."

"So you don't want me to go to college?" I interjected.

"I want you to see that the world for what it is, see who controls it, and I want you to develop your talents to the fullest of your capabilities; I'm not convinced that college is going to do that, at least here. There are other places to go to school and there are other places to work besides Big Cuz. That is what I want you to see. Then you can make your decision."

SamJack pulled over at an old fuel station. He said there was a window of change- we had to wait for the highway police cruiser to pull out from a couple of miles back and pass us. There was 15 minute interval between cruisers. They would then pull out and race ahead to pull over folks who passed them, invariably people of color. He looked at his watch and said that we had two minutes before the car we passed (which I hadn't seen) would emerge to administer what passed for law these days.

Again I was perplexed. "Okay, so where does this trip fit in?" SamJack reached into the console and pulled out a chip.

"Did you bring your term?" I never went anywhere without my terminal. I reached into my jacket and pulled out my Niketec Mobile Video Tablet. "Here put this chip in, but make sure that you have disconnected from everything; your wal netlink, bluetooth, nfc, everything needs to be dark, because there is nothing but air snatchers out here looking for things to swipe."

I shut down all my external connections down and inserted the chip. The system loaded it and up popped a video profile on a company, NGMI:

Company Description- Namibian Graphite Manufacturing, Inc. was incorporated in the Cayman Islands on February 13, 2023 as Kongiste Import Export Inc. On December 14, 2024, it completed a reverse merger transaction with Mumbai Africa International Limited, or MAIL, a company incorporated in the British Virgin Islands on February 1, 2016. The company engages in the manufacture and sale of Graphene based construction materials and other graphene based products. The company offers graphene formulative sheets which are used in the manufacture of protective armor for police and military use; graphene conductive sheets which are base materials for the manufacture of solar photovoltaic panels and graphene beams and arches used in LTSS (lightweight temporary shelter structures). The company sells its products directly to end users that consist of companies in the military and personal

protection industries, solar energy
manufacturers, and LTSS fields. The company
sells its products throughout Europe, in
China, Japan, Australia, Canada, India,
Brazil and South Africa as well as to select
customers in the United States. The company
is based in Ondekaremba, Namibia.

"Are you in an investment club? I thought that the stock markets closed years ago?"

"They are closed", SamJack remarked bitterly, "closed to anyone who didn't already have a substantial investment in them.The day to day market is now run and managed entirely by networks of computers that are named for the companies that built them. Essentially, the market is one big dark pool, and the profits that are generated by the networks create wealth for only those who have enough money invested- what you and I or Titi gets out of it for our retirement fund is barely enough to cover day to day needs- a drop in the bucket compared to what is actually generated."

"Not only that, let's say I did have enough money tomorrow morning- then you have the investment 'good citizen' clauses- a clean arrest record and no entries in government threat databases. Since I fail based on that criteria, no matter how much I amass, I still cannot invest."

"Can't you get your record cleared since you haven't been back?" I offered, hopeful.

"Nope, the government may be required to expunge it in that case, but the stock market is a private entity, so they can keep my record and use it against me...forever."

"So, back to what I gave you. Based on what you read, would you invest in that company or not?"

"I don't know," I replied, hesitating; one minute he had me thinking he was a Biggie Smalls, Titi's resident term for a gangster, next thing I know he flips on me and channels Mark Zuckerberg. I figure that there are a lot of solar panels but they last for 30 years, so I think manufacturing for that product will level off. The market for personal armor for soldiers...well, for anybody is probably a good market, so based on that I would invest in it."

"Okay, you are right and wrong. Here's why: solar panels get replaced regularly because of storms, lightning strikes, power surges caused by solar flares, and such, so the manufacturing for panels will continue to rise. War and law enforcement on the other hand, is being automated, so there are fewer human soldiers and more robotic troops, thus less personal armor. Additionally, there is the trickle down process for technology. Now that graphene has run its course for advanced military applications and been supplanted by composites mined from the Near Earth Asteroid project, graphene will become a material used in everyday household items. The market for which is of course much larger than what this company currently serves. So this is a potential goldmine."

A small carnival of lights raced past as the cruiser shot up the road, ostensibly looking for us. I shook my head and SamJack and I continued my education.

"But you said you can't invest in it."

"Right, but that doesn't mean I can't leverage what I know to make money off of it."

"How?"

"That is what you are going to learn tonight. Not so much so you can follow in my footsteps, more so that you will understand the process of identifying potential money makers early so when you get your shot, you will be able to invest."

"You said I would need a lot of money to invest though."
"You are getting ahead of yourself. Just pay attention tonight. I've explained what I think about this company. Tonight, I have to present it to a group of associates. We will decide whether this or some other company is our next bet."

"How did you find out about this company?"

"Their initials were on the back side of the shields that the guards use at Sykesville Work Camp. One day there was a near riot that broke out; it started between two guys in my group and when the guards rolled in to break up the fight, they beat all of us down and I remember one guard in particular kept hitting me with his shield until I grabbed it; I saw the initials and I was determined to find out what the shield was made of, because if felt like getting hit with a steel pipe, but the guard was swinging it like it was made of paper."

With the pain of that memory SamJack receded into

silence, and pulled out of the abandoned station. I looked out the window, wondering if the journey I was taking would land me in a work camp like my cousin. We got about 5 miles up the road and there on the side of the road, lights ablaze, was the sleek, dark highway cruiser. In front of it was a car with a family full of folks that looked just like us.

Eastpoint Mall maintained the facade of commerce up until 2016, when the oil embargo of 2015 caught up with the east coast of the U.S. The city ceased bus service to anywhere outside of the interstate highway and like that, Eastpoint went from quasi occupied to boarded up. A couple of enterprising churches attempted to set up shop there, but found too that their parishioners preferred to praise Jesus via netlink rather than spend Sunday morning out of their homes. A scion of one of the shipping tycoons of Baltimore finally purchased the mall to maintain it as a tax write off. SamJack's group rented a space in the mall for their monthly gatherings. The remote location allowed for a small sense of security from the omniscient eyes and ears of the city's security apparatus.

I smirked when I counted 12 cars in front of storefront that was completely dark except for the light that was seeping through the outline of the doorway. "I see Titi's rule of 13 has influenced your group." SamJack faced me as he pulled on black gloves. "Mmm-hmm. 13 is our number. Alright, this is time for you to watch. Don't open your mouth to say anything unless you are asked. Don't touch anything, even if someone tries to hand something to you. Just keep your hands in your pockets. Stay with me and watch what I do, and turn off your term and any other device you have on you and leave them in here."

SamJack shut off the car, and reached into the backseat and pulled out a small black bag. He pulled the chip out of my term and wiped it down. "Pull your hood on before you get out too. Even out here, there are always eyes."

As SamJack and I approached the entrance to the meeting, and my mind was inundated with images from the vid shows I watched- smoke filled rooms with old tear drop shaped light bulbs hanging from a wire in the middle of a room. Men wearing funny hats and suits playing with cards that looked like Titi's divination cards; gunfire, police and mayhem. There was always at some point a lot of noise, doors busted open, furniture thrown, arguments and fisticuffs in those scenes. Everything about this moment with SamJack pointed to a similar type of outcome, but the only noise I could discern in the parking lot was the distant sound of traffic. Nothing emanated from the store front except faint light.

When SamJack reached the door, he pressed eye against a keyhole in the door and it flashed green as an ocular scanner identified him. SamJack pulled the door open and motioned for me to follow him inside. The store inside looked gutted; flat gray cement floors, steel pillars traveling up past ancient fluorescent lighting fixtures hanging in disrepair from an un-insulated ceiling. In the middle of the floor about 20 yards away was an area with white tile on which 23 people, from my count, stood behind chairs around a series of folding tables that were pushed together. At each corner of the tiled platform was a black and silver device the size of a suitcase that were all plugged into generator that was quietly humming a few yards behind the platform.

There was a large, bright-eyed Black man at the edge of the platform that motioned for SamJack and me to quicken our pace. SamJack strode up to the man and shook his hand silently and then turned and motioned me over to the two seats at the edge of one of the tables. As soon as SamJack and I stepped over to our seats, blue walls of light sprung up around the platform that joined above our heads above the tables. SamJack and the 12 other primary participants each pulled an ancient terminal out of their respective bags and an equally ancient network cable. In the center of the tables was a networking hub to which everyone connected their terminal. Also attached to the network hub were two modern quantbit drives, presumably to store whatever was entered by the terminals. The men all powered up their terminals and once this was complete, the bright-eyed man motioned for everyone to stand up and then spoke.

"Modupe Ase, Brothers", he said in laughing baritone voice. "I greet you all and all of our newcomers. The participants here are bound to secrecy and by your presence you enter into that covenant with us. We have no name, only a mutual interest in the uplift of our communities and our families. Today we come together to review the fruits of our labor and to choose our next endeavor. Seat #13 will present our next opportunity and then Seat #5 will report on the latest results. Let us proceed."

The thirteen primary men all clapped and then sat down at their terminals.

I sat down and looked around at the men, trying to figure out which one was Seat #5. The seating was not in numerical order. Based on his conversation in the car, I figured that SamJack was Seat#13, but the passive faces of the men at the terminals made it a task to figure out anything else. The blue walls hummed in the background and I in turn watched SamJack, who passively stared at his terminal's screen as it lit up and a window opened that looked like a chat room:

Seat #1: #13, are you ready to proceed?

SamJack's hands sprung to life and he typed:

Seat #13: Most certainly, #1. Greetings, Brothers. The opportunity for this month is NGMI, a graphene manufacturer in Southern Africa. The materials manufactured by this corporation up this point have been limited to the military and energy sectors, but with the automation of ground soldiers and police forces, the company's core target market has been compromised, and that has driven the price of their shares down to 16.52 as of market close yesterday. Here is where our opportunity lies. Graphene production has been limited to the two sectors I mentioned previously, but as of q2 of this year, graphene will receive certification for usage in consumer product manufacturing in both the EU and the NAFTA economic zones. Companies cannot place orders for the material until the certification is received, thus when NGMI released its quarterly report, its numbers looked horrible because its production overhead outpaced its earnings 8 to 1. To analysts and historical market prediction databots, this looked like a classic case of the mismanagement/graft that plagued sub-Saharan mineral and materials interests over the past 50 years. However, when looking at the consumer market, one can find a strong list of companies whom already do business with NGMI as a defense materials vendor that are poised to release products that feature lighter, space age, mark and dent resistant material. This fits the description of graphene. In short, NGMI is poised to explode as a supplier to the consumer product manufacturers.

SamJack's presentation was impressive- and he surprised me because he types way faster than me. I scanned the faces around the table to gauge the reaction from the others. The hum of the blue wall was all that could be heard as the men considered the proposition. Seated across from us were a couple of men who looked as if they were from the East side-they were Latino.

Seat #1: The room is now open for discussion.

I looked around the table. Several of the members were

quietly conferring with the people that they had brought with them. SamJack looked over to me and I gave him the thumbs up. He nodded and turned back to the screen. This was so clinical compared to Titi's various meetings that I had attended. One of her clubs was an investment group, and their raucous meetings were often punctuated with arguments and laughter; but then again, Titi's group's rule was that they only invested in companies that made products they use regularly. So the discussions about stocks usually devolved into arguments about the merits of hair products or food. This was a whole different type of animal. SamJack's screen lit up.

Seat #7: My second and I believe that this is solid prospect. #13, do you have a recommendation for the terms of investment?

Seat #13: As strongly as I feel about this prospect, I recommend that we proceed with the traditional 18 month cycle and standard pot.

Seat #7: But with the scenario that you've laid out, don't you believe this merits a more substantial commitment on our part?

Number Seven was seated three positions down from us; I could hear the click of his terminal's keys when he responded. He was bespectacled, brown skinned and didn't look like he missed any meals whatsoever. After he posted his response to SamJack, he stared down the table at us. SamJack's gaze was still fixed on his workstation as he formulated his response.

Seat #13: #7, I appreciate your unwavering support in this endeavor, but I am of the mind that we have to reel in our assets and reestablish some baselines in regards to our Pot. I like the money as much as the rest of you but I like stability even more. Our success has been built upon our stealth. We register as a nano percentage of the traffic in the market, and I feel that the increases that we have enacted will only serve to make our presence known to those whom we desire to keep out of affairs.

Seat #5: So what are you saying Sam, you want out?

Seat #1: Number Five, please observe the decorum of this assembly and utilize the nomenclature that we have established for the participants.

Number Five sucked his teeth. That's how I knew who he was; and if anyone here fit the description of a gangster, Number Five was it. He had on a suit with a baseball cap, and when he leaned his head against his hand, there was a gleam from the huge wrist terminal he wore. SamJack meanwhile had a look of amusement, but I could see his jaw tensing up. The blue wall hummed as Number Five typed.

Seat #5: My apologies #1 and #13, I simply feel that every time I bring in dough for this group, my work is questioned. I don't want to remind you all that I am the one who got us in with this particular network. All some of y'all give me is bitching and moaning. As much money as I've brought this group, why wouldn't you want more?

160

SamJack shifted in his chair, and his mind shifted to the day he met #5. This was back when he was scrambling on the block, working for Corona. He was in front of a store on the west side, a couple of blocks from the commuter lot, leaning from one foot to the other against the wall of the store. This was the part of the hustle that he had no stomach for; the ceaseless waiting, rain or shine. It unnerved him that a blue lamp's camera was fixed on this corner. He was being watched by those who could use any pretense to swoop down and change the direction of his life. Working on the block meant that one had abrogated control of their destiny to multiple unseen others, a fate that most met with a shrug of resignation. SamJack on the other hand was enraged by that variable. He often said "Anyone who WANTS to be out here has a domesticated hustle. My mind is not built to be on a leash." Today he had no choice, and to top it off, he wasn't alone. Corona had sent over a new kid, another Black kid from the county who Corona wanted checked out by SamJack; "I can't tell if this one is a soldier or spy, Jack. He seems to be doing good work down in E. C. (Ellicott City) working out the warehouse. Tell me what you think."

Sam and the other kid, Troy, rode their bikes over to the store, leaned them against the wall and Sam went inside the store to hand a package to Raj. Raj, in turn, handed Sam a paper bag with a signal grabber inside. SamJack and his brother had been working at a warehouse for Corona when they brought to him the idea of setting up signal grabbing inside the city. Corona was a skeptic; "That shit won't work! What you gonna use to grab the stuff? How are you going to get close enough? How are you going to hide it and transport it once you got it?"

SamJack had a plan- map out the busiest streets in the city used by folks that work at Big CUHS and other large conglomerates in the city; set up kids at random spots during rush hour with signal grabbers near an intersection, and grab the commuter's information using the near field communication protocol to copy transactions off of their phones and tablets. Corona was skeptical until SamJack went out and tested it. It worked beyond their wildest dreams- they were able to snag up to a thousand files each time out.

Corona had SamJack set this up through their network of cities, and soon their gang had half a million files that were random enough that it could not be traced to any one bank or network. A random network tax or texting surcharge that drew fifty cents from each account every month made Corona richer and elevated SamJack to the upper ranks of lieutenants. Corona had plans for SamJack, but SamJack had his own itinerary. The signal grabbing was a confirmation that his ideas could work; but he didn't want to be stuck in Sykesville for the rest of life on account of digital larceny.

Troy had his own ideas too; he was a big kid who was developing into the type of person that was great with results, but details be damned. He hated being out on the block too, but not for the same reasons as SamJack; he'd rather be riding out in a Maserati Bird Cage like the stars do. Like any kid hip to what was going on in the streets, he had heard about Corona, so when he found out that his cousin was managing a rib shack that Corona owned, he begged his cousin to get him a job. Six months of working at the warehouse after school had given Corona a bit of trust in Troy, but the boy's ambition still gave him pause. Corona had sent him up to the city to be checked out by the one person who he trusted to be thorough in his assessment.

SamJack checked the settings on the grabber and made sure the quant chip was securely seated. He then checked his watch; it was about 10 minutes before traffic thickened with commuters headed back to their enclaves. "So what are we doing here?" asked Troy.

"Looking like we are having a good time." replied SamJack.

"We gonna boost from somebody?" SamJack stared flatly into Troy's eyes.

"We don't do shit like that. Did you do dumb shit like that in the warehouse?"

"Oh shit," Troy was impressed. "How did you know that I worked there?"

"I know everything that I need to know about you, and then some," replied SamJack, tersely.

"So who are you?" Troy said, puffing up in response to SamJack's glare.

"I'm the one that knows, and that's all you need to know."

The remainder of their time on the block, SamJack was silent while Troy alternated between singing the latest club chant and bragging about his future wealth. SamJack later told Corona, "In all the movies that my Aunt had me watching, there was always one who messes it up for the rest because they thought they was bigger than everyone else. If you put that boy on anything beyond muscle, that's what he's going to do to you."

Corona's eyes narrowed, trying to discern if what SamJack told him was wisdom or jealousy. "Well what about you? Why wouldn't you be that one?"

"No disrespect Padre, but I plan being out doing my own thing in the world; I can't afford to make any moves that will burn bridges."

SamJack's resolve faltered and he scowled. Troy hadn't changed a bit since that first encounter. His advice to Corona went unheeded; after he got out of Sykesville, he and his brother had left the organization, and Corona had promoted Troy. The results of Troy's more aggressive, glitzy approach initially surpassed anything that SamJack had ever done for Corona, but eventually the very same hustle that led to SamJack's ascension in the group led to Corona's operations being compromised; and Troy was to blame. Now SamJack saw the same prospects on the horizon for this group if Troy's actions weren't curtailed. Soon. Troy had emerged from the collapse of Corona's gang with money, muscle and connections; he set about building his own empire.

SamJack continued pressing his point during the meeting:

Seat #13: Have you bothered to read the law for rogue trading? Or better yet, have you read any of the news stories about rogue

```
trader trials and how they were caught? I
have. They were caught because the volume of
their transactions rose continually over a 24
month period. That is enough time to gather
enough transactions to trip off the network's
transaction filters. Our standard pot,
spread across a diverse portfolio and staying
under a quarter of a million shares,
minimizes the possibility that we lose our
investments.
```

There was a murmur throughout the gathering. I had the feeling this wasn't the first time that my cousin and Number Five had crossed swords. There had been a line drawn and it seemed that most of the participants stood on our side. Even in the midst of the quiet, I could look around the tables and see that the gathering had lost its veneer of civility and tempers were beginning to flux. Number One, as the moderator, was faced with a problem. If he talked, he would violate the protocol of the gathering; yet in this delicate moment, a soothing word was needed in service of the protocol's upkeep. He cleared his throat.

"Brothers, we have reached a fork in a road, or yet a fork has been presented to us. I need not remind you that this endeavor requires single-mindedness, so we can choose our path together, or the fork will be stuck in us."

Some of the men chuckled quietly, but there was no mirth in their responses. Number one however was satisfied and turned back to his terminal.

```
Seat #1:  #5, are you ready to proceed
with your report?
```

Seat#5: Yes, I am. I am importing the
file into the meeting space now.

A file icon popped up on SamJack's screen and then
opened up.

Month #3- ITLX Initial Purchase price:
$35.00 Month #12 Opening: $42.65 Month #18
Closing: $61.58   Gross Div: $11.36 per
Shares sold: 7,777 Shares remaining: 2,223

Around the table, brows were furrowed and the men cut
eyes towards each other around the table. SamJack was again
blank in the face, but he flexed his hands in front of his face
in a series of madras that I knew from Titi's instruction as a
mudra. Bhutadama was a particular position designed to fend
off negative energies. At this point, I had the feeling that
Bhutadama was losing the battle as SamJack's jaw flexed.
Images of mayhem ran amok in my mind. SamJack's screen
lit up again.

Seat #10: This is not adding up. I know
I'm not the only one seeing this shit.

Seat #11: Cosign. My second seat is
looking at these numbers and doing the math
now- just at face value this doesn't add up.

Seat #5: Brothers, there is no doubt in
my mind that you are all accomplished with
the calculator, but I can assure you that the
numbers are correct. You may be missing
several factors.

SamJack turned around to me. He mouthed a figure to me, "1279111.99". I couldn't understand what this number was supposed to mean, but I knew that I better come up with something quick. I said, "hunh?" and SamJack quickly whispered, "look at the screen and figure out which would that number be a product of based on an 18 month investment. This type of math was easy for me. I quickly answered, "35.00". SamJack's nostrils flared, "exactly." He began to type.

Seat #13: It's clear to me that there is a discrepancy between the initial purchase price and the opening. Our Gross dividend should be calculated based on the Initial, not the opening. We clearly laid this out in our bylaws and it seems that this has been overlooked by #5.

Seat #5: Overlooked? Hell no. I went deep, dug deep into my network to set this transaction up? I know which is which- the problem is you niggas is greedy and cheap and don't want to admit it.

Seat #10: Show us the initial transaction slip then. If it says 42, then you can walk out of here.

Seat #1: Number 10, we cannot entertain threats in our midst.

Seat #10: Understood #1, but misappropriation of funds is a bigger no-no for me than telling a jerk what's going to happen if they are misappropriating my funds.

Seat #5: That's it, you ungrateful fucks can forget about me bringing you any more jewels.

Seat #13: Show us the slip, Troy.

Troy stood up suddenly, startling everyone it seemed except SamJack and Number One. He ripped the network cable out of the back of his terminal, and pulled out the chip before handing it to his second seat.

"I ain't gotta sit here and listen to this bullshit. I was doing y'all a favor, and this is what I get? Shit, I know y'all can't do better, but y'all bout to find that out. Let's go D."

Number One's smile was all teeth. "Troy, this can all be resolved with one simple action. Show us the initial transaction slip. I know that this doesn't fall under our normal procedures, but these are extraordinary circumstances and..."

"Fine, Femi, I'ma do that for y'all, but after that, we done."

"It is not on your chip?"

"Naw, I gotta go out to the whip and get it." Femi looked around at the rest of the men and sighed.

"Number 8, please deactivate the jamming field so Number 5 can retrieve the data we requested."

I couldn't believe they were going to let them go. Even I knew that once he was out the door, Number 5 was going to be in the wind. I couldn't see who Number 8 was, but a moment after Number One made the request, the blue walls vanished and once again we were in a bare storefront. Number 5 and his second seat moved towards the exit with calm haste. SamJack's voice stopped them in their tracks. "Naw Troy. Your boy can stay here and I'll walk out with you to get the chip."

SamJack stepped down from the platform and the rest of the men followed. As Troy stood halfway between the men and the door, his demeanor took on the energy of one positioned where walls join. "It would be your punk ass, Sam." He stepped into my cousin's face, and even though Sam was a shade over 6 foot, Troy towered over him. "You wanna walk me out, nigga? Huh?" He leaned into SamJack's face and hissed, "What you gonna do when we get out there and there ain't no other chip? You trying to go back to Sykesville?" He grabbed Sam's collar, and I saw Sam reach into his pocket. He pulled out his hand and reached up clamped something on the side of Troy's coat and pushed him away.

There was a click and the zap cap's quiet whine filled the void as it delivered its message. Troy collapsed and thrashed on the floor, arms and legs akimbo as the current slowly singed him from the inside out. While not lethal, SamJack had seen to that, the device quickly provided Troy with a close up examination of his mortality, one seared nerve ending at a time. The shock pinned his eyelids open, gnarled his hands into claws, and ripped a stuttering scream out the back of his throat. Nobody said a word. SamJack glared impassively at Troy while his second seat, Durant, stood by with teeth and fists clenched, unable to aid his friend. The whine of the zap cap ceased and Troy lay quivering on the ground.

SamJack looked around and said, "Any of y'all could do whatever you want to do- that's the difference between a man and the rest of the animal world; but when you shit on your own kind, steal from your own people, you nothing more than an animal, and you best believe...I will treat you like one."

SamJack took a deep breath and went back to the platform and grabbed his terminal and bag. I strained to hear anything beyond the ragged breathing of the fallen gangster. Troy cast a glance up at SamJack, his dry, bloodshot eyes straining to discern if this was the end of his ordeal. "D, hand me that bag", Troy said to Durant, sounding as if his tongue could not fit in his mouth.

SamJack walked back over to Troy, reached down and Troy flinched; with a click SamJack popped the spent zap cap off of Troy's collar and back into his pocket. SamJack then offered Troy a hand, and the fallen man paused before accepting the offering and wobbling to his feet. He grabbed his bag, reached in it before a not so subtle glance from Number One dissuaded him from pulling out whatever it was he considered an equalizer. He and Durant began to once again make a move towards the exit. Sam turned to Number One and they shared a glance. He nodded to me and promptly spun and walked towards the door. The words that he had spoken seemed to remain suspended in the air of the space; while they gathered their things to leave some of the men still nodded in agreement; but no one raised their voice to speak.

redlining

A MEMORY & A DREAM

BY INDIRAH ESTELLE

It had been about six months since the bomb, and Reginald

looked out over the Harbor at the exact place where his life

was completely altered. Since that day, he had not seen any of

his family, because fate would have it that they were on

vacation, visiting family in Ohio. He was still confused and

sick to his stomach on why his sister didn't go with the

family, or why she had to be within the radius of the blast.

His mind wandered along, and he chuckled as he walked

down the charred sidewalk, as the burnt drywall and

insulation still crunched under his feet; he remembered when he and his friends would come to the card shop every Friday just to blow some steam or just kick it.

Now, it was still unreal to him how things changed so drastically since he was young. Today, he was making his way up to Fayette Street to see if he could get a bus, which at times, he found rather annoying because the new model of buses had neither driver nor wheels. Thus, no one to hear you when you ran after the #15, banging on the side under someone's window; no one to stop the bus and put the knuckleheads off, at least until the police would jump on at the next stop after they received a call.

Everyone's role in society had changed so to speak. Robots controlled the buses once that were dispersed into the city. The bus system had one supervisor, who ironically was well known in Baltimore as the "Running Man". Somehow, he had made his way to the top of the totem pole at The MMOHT (The Mass Movement of Human Transit).

Meanwhile, automation took jobs from a lot of middle class working people, and left them struggling to find work.

Reginald thought about this as he got on the bus and rode through downtown. He found himself staring as a drunken man exiting the bus attempted to prevent himself from falling, but being that the bus is six inches off the ground; his fall was nothing else if not inevitable. Reginald turned away and rode until his thoughts took over his mind completely. The day of the blast, he got called to Vancouver, Washington. He was a FBI agent, and Vancouver was in the midst of a huge standoff that had taken a turn for the worse; now it was a bomb threat. A bank robbery attempt had turned into a hostage situation, which had been going on for about four days. Robots, which were the tellers at the bank, went against the humans, and no one in the city could override the system. Reginald was the best at what he did; he was a top ranking FBI agent, head of a bomb squad and the best negotiator on the east coast. The bank was being held up and in the midst of that the robot workers all went rogue, attacking the head programmer of the bank's workers. Outside of the bank there was police, FBI and SWAT teams. Reginald and three other members of the SWAT team were sent in to negotiate with the robbers. The four men who attempted to rob the bank were being held against their will because the robots were programmed to only recognize workers of the Vancouver Bank behind the counter and clearly they were not them.

As Reginald and his counterparts worked to extract the hostages and override the robot workers to be able to get the robbers out of the hands of the rogue robots, he had gotten word from his head of chief that there had been a deadly explosion back home in Baltimore, Maryland. At that moment, his reality faded as the volume of the programmer's screams increased from the corner of the room; all of a sudden he just wasn't 'there' anymore. His sister Keisha was all he thought about- was she safe? It had been weeks since he had heard anything from her. Was she okay, was she alive?

Realizing that his stop was coming up and the homeless woman was inching her way closer and closer to falling asleep against his shoulder, Reginald popped back to the present, getting a glance of what might have been an old comrade. He rubs his eyes and swiftly pushes the stop box and gets off at Charles and Read Street. He pushes the stop box just in time so the bus can pick up the signal that he wanted to exit. Walking swiftly and anxiously and observing the man standing at a distance to see if it was him, he called out.

"James, is that you?" He turned around with twinkling old brown eyes, and smiled at Reginald as if it was just yesterday they were hanging out and doing what boys did chasing skirts down at the Gallery. James gave him a handshake and pulled him into a warm hug, then pulled him back and examined him. He exclaimed in disbelief.

"Man, it's been about twelve years now, I don't even know what to ask?!"

Reginald chuckled and replied "I could say the say the

same thing. Last I heard you were traveling the world, what brings you home?"

"Man I've been trying to round up my family piece by piece after everything that happened and some personal reasons, you know?"

Reginald replied, "I understand. I'm just so surprised to see you." James just laughed again and looked at him with same boyish charm that they both possessed in their youth. They started to walk down the street. James asked, "What are you doing right now? I really want to catch up on things." Seeing how their lives were dramatically altered since their youth, James felt like he had to see what Reginald had been doing since they last saw each other. Before he could even get an answer out James's hand device rings. Hand "held" cell phones were literally a thing of the past. Cellular chips were sold and were installed into the wrist of the buyer. Everything you needed either showed up in front of you or in the palm of your hand, courtesy of holographic technology. When he answered he spoke in short answers and away from Reginald.

Finally, he hurried the person off the phone and went back to his conversation with his friend. He asked, "Did you want to go downtown?" They walked back over to St. Paul Street and tried to get the bus. The one that went pass seemed to be malfunctioning, speeding without being able to stop. So they looked for a car, they saw an empty one on the corner, and James programmed Federal Hill into the system and sat back.

Reginald asked, "So how's the family. Is anyone still here in the city?" James sighed heavily, glancing out the window. "Well, when the blast happened I was in Port Au Prince doing volunteer work, and I knew everyone was still here." He looked deep thought. "I was so hurt, and I couldn't bring myself to come back, so I decided to keep traveling until that feeling wore off." Reginald could tell that mentally he just went somewhere else. He continued, "I finally came back to see if I could scrape up any answers, or find anything that meant something, I guess." He leaned forward to program to automated cab to stop. They got out, and Reginald looked sadly at James, trying to think of a way to get his mind off the grim past that they both shared. He just shuffled along.

Reginald followed up the steps until they reached the top of Federal Hill. It was one of those moments of silence where a lot can be remembered but still pondering on how much was lost. They both took their places on the bench and just stared over the harbor.

Reginald said, "Ever since the blast I always find myself thinking, 'what if?' like that could have changed anything." He felt the awkward silence in the air. It still felt the same from when they were younger. Sometimes they didn't know what to say to each other, so sometimes just being there listening counted for a lot.

"Now I feel like I can only think forward, like what's next? But I'm a little scared because we all lived like we were invincible, and look what it got us." James smiled, only halfheartedly. He seemed to be looking beyond the skyline.

"We as a people are nothing, seeing that everything and anyone can be taken within a blink of the eye. I've been waking up, praying that yesterday was a dream, and hopefully today isn't true." Reginald put his hands in his face, and his mind began to race.

James spoke slowly, "A close friend told me before she died, 'Dreams are not achievable if you still live with the idea that they won't happen. She also said 'the man who knows nothing he is a humble man. The man who knows nothing clears his mind so he can learn the most.'"

Reginald looked up with utter confusion etched across his face and stared at James. He heard that saying before, ever since he was a little boy but he just couldn't remember from where. Then it hit him. He whispered "Keisha". He stood up and stepped away from James "What happened to her, you know what happened to my sister?" James seemed to shrink, and looked torn between being anxious and confused. He started to stutter "I thought you knew she's gone. She's dead. That was why I came back to the city, for her burial. We had been communicating by writing to each other. She was one of the only people who kept up with me when I traveled, and I kept a good eye on her too." Reginald started to feel his blood boil. He knew he was somewhere between furious and livid, but he didn't know where or whom to be angry with, but that did not stop the feeling from building. James was taken aback by Reginald's anger. He had so many questions but just didn't know what to do or where to start.

Reginald cut in before he could say anything. "How long have you been contacting her?" "It's been years, and you never thought to see how I was doing? I thought we were friends, what was all this about?" Reginald was standing over James now. "Why didn't you ever call or write me, I thought we were boys?" James was just in shock, and the only thing that he could have seemed to find was "I thought you knew." Reginald stared and tried to listen, but there just seemed to be a crack in the planet at that exact moment, and all he could actually digest was white noise ringing in his head. He just fell back into his seat; he didn't know whether to cry or to yell. Just pain and anger overtook him as a whole. James was paralyzed in the moment, so he controlled his every breath and watched Reginald like a hawk. Then, at that exact moment, Reginald jumped back up and started,

"Maybe, I'm the awful person she thought I was, or maybe I was the best brother I could have been. I just can't be understanding this correctly!" He didn't seem to be talking to James but more so projecting his thoughts out loud, and he was just the recipient.

"This just is not real, there has to be something that I'm missing it is just going over my head. Blood is thicker than water. Could this all just be a dream? Would this be my nightmare, or my conscience eating me from the inside out?"

James attempted to interject because it looked Reginald was almost to the verge of insanity. He was wide eyed and just filled with nondescript emotion. Reginald almost started to cry and grabbed James by his shoulders and whispered eerily to him "Wake me up, please I have to dreaming and so none of this is real. Pinch me, maybe our whole lives we've been dreaming and so none of this has been the truth and we have never seen the light." James just stared dumbstruck he didn't know whether to take him seriously or just walk away from the whole situation. The more Reginald spoke of the oddities he felt like the crack in the earth had gotten bigger. He just sat back down and stared without even listening, and a moment later he was up, pacing back and forth in front of his childhood friend pulling his hair and in short, ragged breaths he started to cry. By this time, the sun had started to set, so the sun was already blinding him as James tried to look Reginald in his face. James was just staring and started to drift away. His mind just went somewhere else, but for some odd reason, his daydream brought him back to the same

place. He still couldn't comprehend Reginald for some reason.

Reginald grabbed him "This cannot be life, I know there

is more to it than just this. I need to sleep, or are we sleeping

already?" James couldn't answer him; he was more focused

on the curvy silhouette that was quietly approaching them. In

the setting sunlight, he couldn't see the face of the silhouette,

but he could make out that it was a woman. As the figure

reached the top of the hill, James heart almost stopped. He

was quite sure that it skipped a beat, and his knees almost

gave out. Reginald shook him and yelled louder, but James

just looked ahead as if he had seen a ghost impersonating a

human to be specific. He wanted to speak, but he was still

without his voice, and nothing reached him. Reginald

continued to ramble on "My mind is playing tricks on me, get

me out of here!" He finally looked at James with question in

his eyes, and he just returned him with a blank stare upon his face. Reginald fell onto the bench and just broke down and cried. James did not know what to do he just stared and started to back away. The woman approaching was painfully familiar and smiled at James. She went to Reginald, and with a gentle touch upon his shoulder and that familiar voice rung in his ears said, "I think it's time to wake up."

BRAVEBIRD

BY TONIKA BERKELY

A flash of light from the retinal scanner ran across his eyes as he entered the train. Malik maintained the grip he had on Sofia's hand and guided her over to an empty seat facing the closing doors. A digitized voice resounded overhead.

"Welcome Malik Thomas. Welcome Sofia Thomas. You are on the Redline train, destination Bayview Campus, next stop Allendale." An ad for the newest residential development streamed across the Smartwall opposite from where he sat down and an ad for a new Saturday morning cartoon ran on the board under it. In the center, a Sony 3D LCD monitor broadcast the morning headlines for August 23, 2028.

"Sophie, did Momma take you to the bathroom before we left the house?" Sofia, whose big brown eyes resembled his own, looked him and said matter-of-factly, "No, she said that you were gonna take me before we got on the train."

Damn, I can't believe I forgot that, he thought. "Well, are you doing okay? Do you have to go now?"

"No I'm fine, Daddy." Sofia pulled out her iPod shuffle that she received for her birthday out of her book bag. She hadn't started school yet, but she wanted to carry it with her today as 'practice for school.' She turned on the Shuffle and he could hear Amel Larrieux faintly singing, 'You're a bravebird, from the rarest kind'-- a song Ayn used to hum to her when she was a baby.

The cottony puffs of hair brushed his chin as he leaned in to whisper in his daughter's ear. "Move over closer to me, honey." She glanced up and pulled the white iPod earbud that was closest to Malik out of her ear. "What did you say, Daddy?" the doors had just opened a second earlier at the Allendale station and even though only three people got on the train, it was standing room only. Sofia's book-bag was slouched in the seat next to her.

"Pass your bag to me so someone can sit down." She reached over and grabbed her bag and placed it in her lap.

"You don't want me to hold your bag?"

"No that's okay; I'm a big girl now so I can hold it myself." Malik couldn't help but to chuckle to himself. He couldn't believe that Sofia was five years old. It seemed like yesterday that he had gotten the call while he was teaching a drafting class at Morgan State that Ayn had gone into labor and today, God willing, he was taking his baby girl to register for her first day of kindergarten.

He pulled his iPad out of his briefcase and opened up the panel for Google. "Early futures", he said into the microphone and the website for the school popped up on the screen. He studied each page carefully, hoping that its contents would provide all of the information that he needed to help him feel comfortable with this decision. Is this the right school for Sofia? Will she be able to develop her gifts there? Will they support her on her journey? Will they take her seriously? Even though these questions ran through his head, Malik knew that, unlike other kindergarten programs that he and Ayn researched, this facility's sole purpose was to assist 'special' children with discovering the answers those to questions.

Sofia climbed up on his lap and put her head against his shoulder. Her tiny heels tapped against the side of his knee. They were running out of options as far as school selections were concerned. Public schools in Baltimore City, while staffed with highly qualified teachers, conceded to grounding learning in rote memorization due to the 'Race to the Top' benchmarks and the national Common Core Curriculum standards. Almost twenty years ago, the Archdiocese of Baltimore closed many of the Catholic schools in Baltimore city, but over the years those that remained dwindled down to a few, mostly high schools. Many of the charter schools and private schools in Baltimore City started to experience a resurgence after 2010, but most of the schools were focused in certain magnet programs or became too expensive. He and Ayn tried to enroll Sofia in local Montessori and Waldorf schools but they had reached capacity for this year. This was the only other private school open in Baltimore City that allows for the type of exploration that children like Sofia need. This school also doesn't have geographic boundary restrictions so the fact that they reside in Baltimore County isn't a factor in her attendance. What is a factor in her admission is the number of students allowed in each class. Invitations were sent out statewide for the open house/registration, but students can only be admitted based on a lottery system and the student must be present in order to be eligible for selection. They only have room for 50 new students each year total, kindergarten through 5th grade. Malik knew that if they didn't get in the door before the lottery began, they would need to enroll her at the school near their home by tomorrow and try to get her into the Academy next year.

When he was five, Malik attended Bolton Hill Nursery School which provided the initial research model for Early Futures Academy. He remembered being so excited to be a part of the Children's Think Tank, where he learned how to go to the library and find books about the universe and to 'travel to other planets while laying still'. He looked at the picture of the headmistress on the school's homepage. She looked very similar to how he remembered her when he was younger: very light blonde hair- almost platinum, deep set crystal blue eyes, girlish looking face. She had published extensively on futures teaching and childhood perceptions of the future, cosmology, and mythology and opened the Early

Futures Academy as a research-based educational center a few years ago. The Academy uses the personal learning environment model, where student learning is constructed from information and resources that they select and organize. There is a minimum of two teachers in each classroom and notable professors from the Maryland Institute College of Art and the Peabody Conservatory are also employed to guide instruction.

Malik and his firm designed the building a few years ago and the final product came out better than he'd hoped for. It is the first elementary school campus of its kind in the Mid-Atlantic. The circular buildings are placed around a series of courtyards which are designed for outdoor instruction with exterior Smartwalls. A meditation labyrinth is available for student's use and is located at the center of the building. A retractable awning hydraulically extends to cover the entire school in case of rain or extreme weather. There are also specialized rooms within the building to help students destimulate or process learning material, specifically subterranean meditation rooms and auditory amplification rooms (with sunken Bose PhaseGuide speakers). The school is powered by a self-sustaining hydroelectric and geothermal heating system. Its tanks collect rainwater and snow from cisterns in the roof or water from the ground, filters the water and supplies water and energy to the entire campus.

One day, Malik was in the kitchen getting caught up with the morning's news on his Ipad, when he saw that the date set for the open house for Early Futures Academy was in August. "I don't see why this is so important to you", Ayn said. "She's only starting kindergarten. It's not like this is her last year of middle school and she needs to get into a magnet program next year. Besides could we really afford to send her to a school like that?"

"Where is this coming from? Haven't you seen what's been happening with our daughter for the past year?

"Of course, I see it…"

"Then you know that she isn't an average five year old," he snapped. Hell, the admissions counselor even confirmed it. She's special, Ayn."

"Don't you think I know that?" she said, slamming the coffee carafe on the table. Her eyes started to glaze over and water pooled on her lower eyelid. "I'm scared. I feel like I don't know how to help her."

Malik rose from his chair and walked over to Ayn who was looking out the window. He placed his hands on her shoulders. "Baby, I know you're scared for her, but this window has been opened for her now, just like it was for me at her age. Only it wasn't held open for very long. In middle school and high school, I was on my own." Ayn turned around to look at him. The somber look in his eyes pulled her away from the tempest that started growing inside her.

"I could never focus in class so I started getting in trouble for getting smart with the teacher or picking fights with other students. Eventually, they placed me in Special Ed because I was diagnosed with ADD and dyslexia. I started to feel like I didn't fit in anywhere: not with my boys or my family. My grades started slipping in every subject except Art and Math. In 9th grade, I started getting into drawing, especially buildings and bridges. Ayn, I could flip through different architecture books, pick a random structure and draft plans of it after only looking at it once." He noticed that Ayn, who had been shaking 15 minutes earlier, was now completely still. "Sure everything worked out. I graduated from high school and got into Morgan, but there were plenty of times when it almost didn't. I just don't want Sofia to go through what I did: the isolation, the fear, feeling like you're defective…that something is wrong with you, yet knowing that there isn't."

He put his arms around Ayn and held her tightly. "All I ask is that you remain open to this. We need to do whatever we can to give her a fighting chance." He wiped the tears from her wet cheeks. "Okay?"

"Okay," she sniffed.

The car lurched forward causing Malik to tap his forehead on the behind of the large woman standing directly in front of him. She turned around to cut him with her eyes. "Sorry," he said sheepishly. The trains were so congested this time of morning. It reminded him of when he was a child and he went to visit the Smithsonian in DC, either on a class trip or if he was visiting the National Building Museum, during rush hour. People would pour in through each of the doors for the first few minutes, seemingly endless streams of bodies, packing themselves close to each other like cattle on railway cars, trying to fit in any space with an arm for a briefcase or a backpack. People who were lucky enough to find seats would experience some reprieve, but the ones sitting in the aisles were usually challenged with having someone's large book bag in their face or resigned to the threat of being constantly elbowed by people standing in the aisles. It would be difficult for them to navigate their way through the crowd to get back to the doors to get out once they arrived at their station. So it was important that when they came to the station before theirs, he was able to remain in a position that they could flow out quickly, but in a way that he wouldn't lose Sofia in the rush. This confusion around the number of people packed into the cars occasionally caused arguments between the passengers. Last year, on more than one occasion, fights broke out at the Howard Street rail station due to the lack of trains running there and at Lexington Market. Once the doors were opened to let people off the train, sometimes they would close too quickly in order to stay on schedule with getting to the next stop. And if you weren't fast enough, you'd get left behind on the platform or stay on the train a little longer than expected. Malik was definitely trying to avoid this, so he had to be able to get off the train at the right time. Otherwise, his whole day would be ruined; he'd miss his stop, would be late for work, and would miss their opportunity for registration.

Sofia also wasn't comfortable being in crowded places for long. A few months ago, Malik and Ayn took Sofia to a quiet restaurant in Inner Harbor East to celebrate her birthday. Within five minutes of arriving, she started to squirm in her seat, hold her ears and kick the table with her feet.

She began to cry and began screaming, "It's too loud. It's too loud! There's too many people talking, stop them from talking!"

Malik picked her up and hurriedly ushered her out of the restaurant with her mom in tow. "What's the matter, honey?" he asked.

"They were talking really, really loud and it was hard for me to hear in my own head," she said.

"What were they saying honey?"

"All kinds of things. One man kept talking about his wife, the man that was behind us was really, really scared about money. But all of them, I could hear all of their voices.

All at the same time, it was so noisy. Daddy, can we just please go home?" she whimpered.

Malik looked at her Ayn, and walked back into the restaurant to speak to the maitre d' about their reservation. A large man that Malik noticed was sitting at the table behind them was standing in front of the waiter with his arms crossed and his face growing redder by the second.

"What do you mean my credit card was declined? Did you run it again? How dare you embarrass me in front of all these people! I'm never coming here again and I will make sure that everyone I know never sets foot in this restaurant!"

The Maitre d' calmly asked the man to follow him and they stepped into another room behind the foyer. Malik tapped the waiter on the shoulder. "Excuse me? Can you let the Maitre d' know that we will be canceling our reservation? Thanks." He couldn't help but wonder if maybe Sofia had heard those voices in her head or maybe she was just acting out because she wanted to go to Panera Bread instead.

Malik and Ayn decided to have Sofia tested by a family psychologist, who determined that she just had a vivid and lively imagination, like any other five-year-old girl. After the restaurant incident and another one in a shopping mall, Malik decided that maybe he should start training her in some of the techniques that he learned while he was at Bolton Hill.

"Now what you want to do is imagine there's a giant beam of white light that comes down to the top of your head. I want you to take this light and move it over your head, down in front of your knees, and underneath of you until it reaches back to the top of your head. Then move the light around your right side and your left side until they meet in the middle. Now you're totally protected, okay?"

Malik looked at Sofia and watched her movements as she guided her hands over her head, mimicking the movements that he showed her. When she was finished she opened her eyes and said "Okay, Daddy."

Before they would go out, he would instruct her on how to shield herself properly. He would take her to places like the supermarket and to the park and to libraries, just to see if it worked. Over time, she remembered how to do the process herself and started to hear the voices less and less. Malik knew that the shielding technique would come in handy when she was ready to learn astral projection or 'travel to other planets while laying still'; one of the techniques that students can learn and develop when you go to the Academy. He also bought her the iPod as an extra defensive mechanism to distract her from the 'noise'.

"Daddy?"

"Yes, honey?"

"I have to go to the bathroom."

"You mean right now?"

"Yes."

"Honey, can you wait a few more minutes? Our stop is two stations away."

"No, Daddy! I have to go right now," she whimpered.

Damn. He had to find a place to take her, but where?

"If I get off the train, I'll lose a half-hour and we'll miss registration," he thought. He also didn't want his daughter to suffer the humiliation of sitting in and smelling like urine for the rest of the train ride back home.

"If this facial recognition camera, or worse a transit cop, spots us, I'm not going to look forward to explaining to Ayn why I'm in jail and our daughter is meeting with a caseworker at DSS. We gotta do this now or my day is shot. Maybe somewhere on the train..."

Malik looked around for an covert location and spotted it. The new trains were constructed with a few wheelchair accessible sections to keep parked chairs out of the aisles. Smartwalls were placed on both sides of the front of this section of the car, making only the head of the person sitting in the chair visible. The seat benches are collapsible to allow for overflow seating if wheelchair placement isn't needed. If I stand in the aisle front of her, she can crouch down and go.

He looked down at the quarter-filled coffee cup in his hand

and swallowed the contents in one gulp. There were five

people left in the car, but they were disbursed throughout the

forward section.

"Come on, sweetheart." He stood up, took Sofia's book-

bag and his briefcase in one hand, clutched her hand in the

other and walked towards the back of the car. The black glass

orb mounted on the ceiling twitched inside as they moved

down the aisle. The wheelchair compartment was positioned

just outside the boundary of the camera's blind spot. They sat

on the bench within the compartment and he handed the

coffee cup to Sofia.

"Okay, sweetie, I want you to listen to Daddy. When I

say, I want you to use the potty in this cup. Okay?"

Sofia's fixed gaze soured to disgust then shifted to

compliance. They had to make this quick because the train

would be stopping at State Center within the next two

minutes. Malik placed his daughter's pack between his feet and opened his briefcase to take out his company's quarterly report newsletter. Sofia was on her knees with her arm behind her and her other hand holding the edge of the bench.

He flipped the newsletter open to the center and whispered, "Now." He heard a slight patter of liquid hitting the bottom of the cup as he looked at the black orb on the ceiling. It remained still, either focused on his reading the newspaper or on the aisle facing the front section of the car. When she finished, she sat back down on the bench. She looked sheepishly at Malik and turned away to look out the tinted window.

Malik picked up Sofia and walked to the other side of the wheelchair compartment and stood by the doors.

"I'm tired, Daddy," Sofia yawned. "When are we going to get to my new school?"

"We'll be there soon enough, the school is a few blocks away from here," Malik said.

"Next stop, State Center," the digitized voice announced. Malik felt himself lurch forward as the crowd clustered around him like metal fragments on a magnet. A woman standing behind him pressed against him, almost knocking Sofia out of the crook of his arm. "'Scuse me. I'm sorry; I'm just tryin' to get off this thing before the doors close." He braced himself once the train came to a halt. The doors quickly slid open and Malik felt himself and Sofia being carried by the momentum of the crowd out the door.

Fortunately, there weren't as many people waiting to get on the train, so he filed in line to get on the escalators to ascend to the street level. The sunshine warmed the top of his head when he reached the summit of the escalator. Malik looked down to check his watch. The registration for the lottery closes in five minutes. He picked up Sofia and ran down the block towards Martin Luther King, Jr. Boulevard, cutting down a side street in front of Bolton Hill Towers.

There was no oncoming traffic on his side of the street, so he bolted to the median and waited for a few hybrid cars to pass before running across E. Preston Street. He feel his clothes getting damp on his chest and under his armpits, as he bounced Sofia on one hip and gripped their bags in the other as he sprinted across the parking lot into the building. He slowed down at the foyer entrance to allow the light to flash across his eyes before he headed towards the sign marked, "Open House Reception".

"Welcome to Early Futures Academy, Mr. Malik Thomas and Miss Sofia Thomas, where the future begins now."

Malik smiled and thought, "All I know is, if she wins this lottery, her momma is bringing her to school from now on."

(This story is dedicated to Ms. Heidi Gustafson, the children at Bolton Hill Nursery School and all students who've participated in the Children's Think Tank.)

THE PRICE OF RIBBON

BY DEVLON WADDELL

Ribbon has become quite the commodity. When I bought my first typewriter, it was merely for aesthetic purposes. I had not intended to use it; my netbook and PC were the tools with which I existed in my chosen trade. Save the failing of my vision and dexterity, my mobile phone would have likely taken the place of those other word processors.

The typewriter was to be situated solemnly in my office, as homage to the long forgotten writers who had toiled away the years, stroke by stroke, liquid paper in tow, penning the truest literature. And it was my belief that in order to truly honor those who had preceded me in this the noblest of all professions, a typewriter–any typewriter not discarded–must be fully functioning; ribbon and all.

I had the tendency to live at least a decade behind most technological advancements. The PC- ten years late; email-ten years late; social media, smart phones, flat screens, HIDS (holographic image display systems)-ten years behind the times. Comfort in my living in the world of the obsolete had set in so that I would no longer effort any attempt at maintaining any relationship with the Jones family. Still, I have always, with great vehemence, refused to subject myself to any of the abhorrent variations of electronic reading devices that flooded society at the turn of the millennium. I saw no greater discourteousness to the literati.

I had once been interviewed by a true champion of the literary world regarding the then current state of publishing. I remember distinctly our exchange about the ridiculousness of books on small electronic devices. We laughed at such a notion. Not long after the interview, he donated his extensive collection of independently published work and replaced as much of his library as he could with all manner of e-crap.

It was after he had sold his soul to the technological devil that I began to covet books–words printed on paper, bound by thread, covered in linen or leather–books. At about the same time in my narrative, I came to know of a place, The Book Thing, where one could donate and take whichever and however many books he wanted. It was an old, ugly warehouse with a hand painted sign and homemade bookshelves that sat in a bad part of town --my part of town.

It was only open on weekends, and for a good while, I could be found every weekend wandering the aisles, combing the shelves for anything old and or interesting. Somewhere between collecting and hoarding, I started to litter my home with titles, too many to list. It seems that those weeks moving into months, then years that I spent at The Book Thing would work toward foreshadowing the reclusive future that I had lamented as a child.

That old, ugly warehouse stands vacant now. On the surface, the acquisition of that property seems to have been one of CUHS's less strategic purchases, as it is a purchase that did not cover the ten square-block minimum usually procured by the University systems. Oddly enough, it stands alone geographically as a property of that organization. The fact that the area is gated for protection of the property serves as little solace for the few, yet holding fast, waiting patiently for the promised gentrification of my hood. Those homeowners are indeed a brave set of community members; delusional, but brave, nonetheless.

I'm sure that it was the extraction of such a gem from my neighborhood that further cemented my covetousness and acted as the catalyst to my technological regression. I have become a caricature of a writer. I am now Forrester or that guy who Forrester found. Seated at my desk, a desk that's tucked under the small window in my small, dim apartment, I find myself searching for the exact combination of words to convey a notion that yet exists.

CAJA CALIENTE

BY JASON HARRIS

TRANSLATION BY MARIALUZ CASTRO-JOHNSON

El hombre gritó mientras se tambaleaba al borde de la acera en Broadway y New Orleans. "Edificios grandes, brillantes, malditos. No puedo ver mierda, yo no sé ni por dónde está la tienda de licores... ¿venden Schlitz ahí? ", se preguntó, señalando una de las fachadas brillantes de la Villa Universitaria Médico Eastside.

La estatura, la curvatura recatada de las vigas y el vidrio imparten un aire de confianza en las modalidades de curación de vanguardia que contiene, al menos para los visionarios responsables de su creación. En realidad, era demasiado grande para representar curación, mejor imaginar el lucro, la función prevista socavada por la escala dominante de la escuela.

En medio de todo queda 1825 E. Calle Monumento. En el mapa de la Universidad, el edificio está identificado como Edificio 77, pero en las calles del Este de Baltimore se le conoce simplemente como "Hot Box" ... la caja caliente.

Stella Koffla-Herrera se sentó en las entrañas de la caja caliente, en un estado de pánico. Su número de casos no eran muchos, pero las palabras de su conversación por la mañana con Roger sonaban en sus oídos. "Stell, yo no necesito que los ames, te necesito para solucionar sus vidas, y documentarlo ... empezando por el archivo de Cabrera." Dio unos golpecitos con los dedos, esperando a que el efecto calmante de su Camophedrine™ se producirá, La intersección en su mapa moral donde su desdén por los dictados de las empresas atravesó su necesidad de participar en el servicio a la comunidad estaba llena de decisiones pendientes. Mirabel Cabrera se había convertido, como Roger tan alegremente había dicho: "una arruga que se necesita planchar. " La intención de la Universidad de declarar su proyecto de rejuvenecimiento de la zona de 25 años un éxito estaba en sus etapas finales, y casos como el de Mirabel podría hacer o romper el valor cuantitativo de los informes que planeaban publicar.

"Ronny". El miró desde su teléfono y frunció el ceño. "Parece que acabas de terminar un triatlón, ¿estás bien?" Se rió Mirabel y pensó: apenas. Sus contracciones venían todavía cada 15 minutos, pero cuando llegaban, se sentían como si trajeren cuatro maletas. Su Nana había sugerido ir a la tienda a comprar pan, e incluso le dio dinero en efectivo, pero pronto se quedó muda cuando le pidió Mirabel que caminara con ella. Lo único que quería hacer era comprar minutos para su teléfono para poder llamar a Oscar.

"Ronny, necesito unos minutos y ..." se aferró a la mesa y jadeaba con la llegada de una contracción.

"Y tengo que sentarme un poco."

"Sentarte?"

" Sí, maldita sea, sentarme. "

" ¿Qué, vas a tener un bebé o algo? "Mirabel frunció el ceño como respuesta.

Rujrajnee la miró pensativamente mientras abría el área del cajero y deslizó una silla.

"¿Cuántos minutos?"

"400", ella respondió deslizando un billete antiguo en la ranura. Rujrajnee suspiró, lo que era demasiada emoción para él-Mira lucia parecía como si ella pudiera tener el bebé aquí.

"Mira, ¿quieres que llame a alguien para ti?"

Mirabel se sentó rápidamente. "¡Por supuesto que no! Es por eso que compré esos minutos, tengo algunos amigos que llamar ."

Ella sostuvo su teléfono en parte frontal del escáner de autentificación en el mostrador. Ronny entró su orden y los minutos se añadieron a su cuenta.

Ronny podía ver el miedo en su mirada, inicialmente esperaba que pudiera atribuirse al hecho de que ella estaba en algún tipo de malestar y no porque ella estaba en algún tipo de problema, pero el hecho de utilizar cuentas legadas para comprar cosas le indico que no sólo estaba embarazada, el bebé estaba en riesgo. Había visto su negocio reducir con la "reubicación" de sus clientes. El detalle de seguridad del

Centro Médico fueron las últimas personas que quería hojeando su tienda, y esto era el tipo de escenario que justamente que llamaban su atención. Ronny tenía sus propios problemas suficientes.

"Qué tipo de mundo le espera al bebe", reflexionó Mirabel.

"¿Eh, oh, sí, así que todos cometemos errores. ¡Espera! Me salió mal", Ronny se sintió avergonzado.

"No te sientas mal Ronny, por lo menos tuviste el valor de decirlo, todos los demás a mi alrededor me están tratando como si yo cometí un error. Pero no lo hice, fue mi decisión."

Mirabel cautelarmente se irguió sobre sus pies. "Ronny, dame un trapeador".

"Un trapeador?" Ronny estaba confundido, no recuerdo haber escuchado algo caerse o romperse.

"Mira, ¿sabes el viejo dicho: Usted lo rompe lo compra."

Eso provocó una carcajada de la joven.

"Buena suerte encontrando líquido amniótico en tu inventario. Mi agua se acaba de romper." Contracción. Aliento. Mueca de dolor. Risita. Mientras que el empleado buscaba un trapeador, Mirabel se apoyó en el mostrador y le envía a Oscar, su novio, un v-texto rápido. 'Bebe', comenzó.

"Llego el momento."

Stella se detuvo en la acera y miró la pantalla en su workbook. El id-bot había escaneado y encontró que el ID de Mirabel, estaba presente en la dirección, 2625 Este Monumento Street. Desde la creación de la ley nacional de identidad hace más de 40 años, ha sido ilegal estar fuera de casa sin su Identificación biométrica emitida por TSA, haciendo que la utilidad de Id-bot, en un principio patentado como una aplicación de medios sociales para uso en lugares muy concurridos como un estadio o un desfile, se use como el localizador de facto del gobierno y las entidades corporativas.

Durante la segunda década del siglo, la aplicación Id-bot fue una herramienta fundamental para los movimientos sociales, utilizadas por los grupos en todo el mundo para organizar marchas de protesta y actos de gran escala de la desobediencia civil. Stella encontraba a menudo la ironía en que la misma aplicación que utilizaba como un adolescente en Grecia durante la guerra de la Unión Europea de 2035, ahora era su herramienta favorita como una "cazadora de recompensas benigna", como a menudo se refería a sí misma.

Stella se frotó el templo, no había visto Mirabel en dos meses, y Mirabel no había llamado hasta ayer.

Mirabel dejó un vmail sucinta, "Stella, en serio, no puedo confiar en ti ... ya sabes por qué. ¡No me llames más!" Blip. En la base de datos de la Universidad, Stella vio que los fondos públicos de asistencia de Maribel fueron congelados, y el archivo de la familia estaba marcada "reubicación necesario", porque dos de los primos de Mirabel, César y Alejandro, indicaron su residencia principal como 2625 Monumento del Este. Ambos habían regresado a casa de la cárcel y fueron identificados como portadores de la enfermedad de la Bahía. Ahora estaba de pie en el porche de la casa de los Favor, escuchando como Google, Rottweiler de la familia, gritaba y pateaba el interior de la puerta principal.

Manuela Cabrera no podía creerlo. Volvió a mirar el canal de seguridad en su TV y no podía creer que la chica tuvo el descaro de estar de pie en su porche. Su vmail fue inundado con mensajes de la oficina del anexo de Investigación para asistencia de reubicación.

"Estos hijos de puta creen que es un hecho," ella hervía mientras deambulaba hacia la puerta. Manuela tomó Google por el cuello y lo espantó por las escaleras del sótano.

Después, llama a Dell, a su hermano.

"Juan, asegúrese de que Mira se que? arriba, tengo que bregar con la puerta."

La sonrisa de Manuela Cabrera cuando abrió la puerta la desarmo.

"Bueno, Sra. Stella, ¿la escuela la envió aquí para que nos ayude a los ilegales empacar?" La sonrisa se volvió fría.

"La señora Cabrera, yo-o-o, sé que esto es difícil, pero estoy aquí para ayudar."

Manuela levantó el dedo," ¿Y cómo es eso? Con vales de mudanza?"

La mente de Stella estaba en blanco mientras la mujer mayor salió al porche. "Déjame decirte algo, mi familia ha sido PROPIETARIOS de esta casa desde hace 51 años. Desde 05 de junio 1977, para ser exacto. Cuatro generaciones de Cabreras han vivido aquí, y otros cuatro lo harán, si usted, de la Universidad, o quien sea le guste o no".

"No quiero que usted tenga que salir, Señora Cabrera," intervino Stella.

"Puede ser que lo quieres, pero ¿tú quién eres? Tú eres el sacerdote a su traficante de esclavos, viniendo aquí hablando de ayudar, pero ¿dónde estabas cuando la familia González fue 'trasladada'? ¿La familia Mota? ¿Los Portillos?"

Manuela ubico su oreja delante de la cara de Stella para efecto. "Usted habla de trabajar duro para ayudar, pero cuando las familias necesitaban ayuda, ¿dónde estabas?" clavando a Stella con el dedo.

"Ustedes tienen el descaro de andar hablando de 'No en mi patio', mientras nos roban las casas bajo nuestras narices. Bueno ¿adivinen qué perra, no en mi patio, casa, donde sea. No quiero verte por aquí, porque todo lo que has hecho es traer problemas." La puerta no terminaba de cerrarse a golpe antes de que las lágrimas de Stella cayeran.

Manuela volvió a abrir la puerta por un momento para gritar:"¿Qué clase de persona congelaría la tarjeta de servicios sociales de una persona cuando se estaba comprando vitaminas para el embarazo? "

Óscar se bajó del autobús y cruzaba la calle a la tienda cuando vio el coche. Era conocido, pero que no podía traer a su mente quién era hasta que vio al conductor. Era aquella mujer de la Universidad que solía siempre estar alrededor de Mirabel. No podía ser una coincidencia que se encontraba en la misma cuadra.

"Es por eso que no puedo quedarme aquí", esta gente de

la Universidad es maldita, " reflexionó. Quería llegar a la tienda, encontrar a Mira, y conseguir un aventón de su primo donde Titi Mirabella en Heights Park. Mira podría tener el bebé donde Titi y luego se podría encontrar la manera de tratarla con las cosas desde allí. Oscar se detuvo para llamar un taxi ilegal . "Maldita sea", dijo él a la vez que el vmail volvió a surgir.

"Tú eres Oscar, ¿verdad?" Él no había visto al llegar.

"Sí, ya sé quién eres tú también, y si yo fuera usted, me diera la vuelta para volver al coche."

"Yo sé que Mirabel y su familia están molestos, pero la única manera que puedo ayudar es si usted me lo permite, porque hay otras personas con quienes trabajo que no se preocupan por ella como yo. "Stella luchó dentro de sí misma por sentirse intimidada por la presencia de la joven. Óscar la miró intensamente y entró en la tienda, cerrando la puerta detrás de él. Mirabel se sintió aliviada.

Oscar agarró el trapeador que Mirabel llevaba y miró a Ronny, "¿Qué diablos es esto?"

"Mi agua se rompió." A la vez que Oscar acabó rápidamente con el trapeador, la puerta se abrió de nuevo.

Las piernas de Mirabel quedaron inertes.

"Oscar tenemos que irnos ahora."

Stella se armó de valor al entrar a la tienda, "Mirabel, sé que no quieres hacerle daño a su familia, pero no se puede tener a este niño en la calle ..."

"¿En la calle?" Mirabel gritó. "¿Así que quieres que yo vaya a su hospital, para que me llenen de drogas, se lleven a mi bebé y me manden a mí y a mi familia al condado? Oscar ... "

Oscar puso el trapeador a un lado y llamó a su primo: "¿Dónde estás, hombre? Guay, estamos en Lakewood y Fayette. Sí; Al otro lado de la estación" Oscar tomó suavemente a Mirabel por la cintura con una mano y agarró su mochila con la otra. "¿Quieres ayudar?", le dijo a Stella ", abre la puerta." Stella abrió la puerta, sus ojos se encontraron con los de Mirabel, mientras ella salía. "Me gustaría que me dejaras ayudarte." Mirabel se volvió hacia ella justo antes de que se metiera en el taxi. "Usted lo acaba de hacer." Con esto se cerró la puerta y el coche se alejo.

REDLINES

BY JASON HARRIS

First in Titi Mirabella's mind was the fleeting question of
whether or not someone would be kicking her door down,
which was standard paranoia that accompanied anything that
she undertook at the behest of her nephews. In comparison to
some of what her nephew SamJack termed 'maneuvers', this
was downright boring. Yet, when she took off her Mama-
Sista-Elder glasses, the risks were apparent. First off, SamJack
and his brother Sedrick were seemingly always 'persons of
interest' to law enforcement officials. However, they couldn't
be boxed in under the typical 5 o' clock webcast police cam
flotsam- they were more John Henry meets Gaspar Yanga

meets Reginald Lewis- men who were raised and wired for success and unapologetic therein.

The more pressing reality for Titi was that home birth was illegal in the North American Union, and here, Titi was in the shadow of the Consolidated University Hospital System's (CUHS) North Campus, setting up her house as a birthing center.

Her nephew's childhood friend, Oscar, reached the CUHS East Campus stop on the red line, got off of the bus, and was crossing the street to the store when he saw the car. It was familiar, but he couldn't pull into his mind who it was until he saw the driver. It was that woman from the University that used to always hang around his girlfriend, Mirabel. It couldn't be a coincidence that she was posted up on the same block. "Ooh, that's why I can't stay around here, these CUHS folks are crazy," he mused. He wanted to get to the store, scoop Mira, and catch a hack over to Titi Mirabella's in Park Heights. Mira would have the baby at Titi's and then they could figure out how to deal with things from there. Oscar stopped to call the hack. "Damn," he said as the vmail came up again.

"You are Oscar, right?" He hadn't seen her walk up.

"Yes, I know who you are too, and if I were you, I'd get right back in the car."

"Look, I know Mirabel and her family are angry, but the only way I can help, Oscar, is if you let me, because there are other people I work with who don't care about her like I do." Stella cursed herself on the inside for being so close to tears. Oscar glared and walked into the store, closing the door behind him.

Mirabel was relieved when Oscar arrived.

Oscar grabbed the mop Mira was holding and looked at the store keeper shouting, "What the hell is this?"

"My water broke," Mira interjected before Oscar went ballistic. As Oscar quickly wiped the floor, the door opened again. Mira's legs went limp.

"Oscar we need to leave now."

Stella steeled herself, "Mira, I know you don't want to

hurt your family, but you can't just have this child in the street..."

"In the street?" Mira yelled. "So you want me to go to your hospital, so they can stick me full of drugs, take my baby and send me and my family out to the county? Isn't that the plan, Stella?"

While the case worker stood by mute, Oscar leaned the mop against a rack of potato chips and called the hack,

"Where are you man? Cool, we are at Lakewood and Fayette...yeah that one. Two minutes? Good." Oscar gently took Mirabel by the waist with one hand and grabbed her backpack with the other.

"You want to help?" he said to Stella, "then get the door." Stella pushed the door open, her eyes meeting Mira's as she walked out.

"I wish you would let me help." Mira turned to her just before she got into the cab. "You just did."

With that the door to the bodega shut and Stella was left to contemplate the fate of another 'case' where the truth didn't fit inside the checkboxes on the file.

Titi sighed, rose from her desk and crossed the room to light some incense. She chuckled, as her first impulse was to look for a match. Scraping the match across the flint left a faint red mark that she squinted to look for each time she called upon fire to assist her. After all this time, fire sticks remained her preferred mode of conflagration. Right now, sage had to be burned to prepare the space for Oscar's pregnant girlfriend. As she walked around the space distributing the smoke from the sage to various nooks and crannies of her house, the Skype tone sounded. She hurried over towards her desk and Dona Maria's face and name popped up. She pointed the mouse at the screen to answer the call. "Hola Titi, tengo que hablar rápidamente porque tengo una emergencia."

"La Dona, se apresura por favor, Mira y Oscar estará aquí pronto."

"No, Ése es porqué le estoy llamando. Mi madre es mismo

enfermo y tengo que atender a ella."

Titi was breathless- she certainly knew enough about catching babies, but Mirabel was expecting Dona Maria to be present, emergency or not.

Dona continued, "Llamé a mi amiga hacia fuera en el condado que es muy experimentado y ella tiene acordó ayudar." (I called my friend out in the county who is very experienced and she has agreed to help.)

Titi was so flustered her Spanish failed her, "Dona, Mira va a ser muy incómodo con un extranjero y Oscar...girl you do NOT want to cross him!"

"Titi, debo ir, su nombre es Sandra y tengo emailed su información a usted. Lo siento que no puedo estar allí hoy." (Titi, I must go, her name is Sandra and I have emailed her information to you. I am sorry I cannot be there today.) The screen went blank.

Titi was livid. "Maneuvers", she muttered as she quickly pulled up the information for Dona's stand-in and called SamJack. While Titi could be reasonably sure that she could randomly stop by her nephew's store on Aisquith and see

Sedrick, she never quite knew where her other nephew would

be. Her only assurance that SamJack was not out of town was

the fact that his childhood friend Oscar was on the verge of

being a Father.

SamJack answered on the first ring. "Mi-Mi, Ti-Ti, what

you need from a Brother like me-me?" he singsonged. On

screen, Titi couldn't decide if he was posing as a fashion

designer or an undertaker. "Looking clean there, Sammy".

He furrowed his brow, "You sweet talking me Titi,

what's up?'"

"Look, mister chief of this and that, I appreciate that

your legendary hustler instincts are still first rate, but right

now I need for you to pick someone up ASAP- I am texting

the address to your GPS now. Her name is Sandra. Pick her

up and bring her to the house. She's going to catch Oscar's

baby."

With his impeccably tailored black suit, shirt and tie,

SamJack was everything and nothing that Titi explained to

Sandra on Skype. A perfect black cocktail dress- that was what she pictured herself wearing as she peered through the peephole at the man whom Titi described to her as part 'shadow and shark'.

To her credit, when Titi said that, Sandra overrode her usual feel good granola instincts to say, "Why in the hell are you sending a shadowy shark to pick up a woman?"

Titi backtracked from her hyperbole enough to say "I said that so you wouldn't be intimidated, but he is my nephew and you are in good hands."

Now the shadow stood on her stoop.

"Are you always this dapper when you pick a girl up?" she quipped as she opened the door. SamJack placed the bait right back at her feet.

"Does a CEO stop being a CEO when running errands? More importantly, do you have your baby-catching tools?"

"Yes, I'm ready, but I'd really prefer to drive and follow you to Titi's."

SamJack snorted. "Nope. I'm your fastest and safest

route to Titi's, and I will make sure a car is sent to bring you home. Let's go, this little boy isn't working on our clock."

Titi's mind was adrift a sea of tangents. Oscar and Mirabel had arrived in a state of panic after talking to Dona on their way over to the house. This is where Titi's experience as a doula kicked in - she gave Oscar a bag of food and supplies to take to the room where Mirabel would labor. Titi then sat Mira down and gave her a foot massage and let her know that SamJack was on the way with Sandra. "Calm the mother so that she can, in turn, get out of the way of her body, and let it do the work." So said Ina Gay Franklin when Titi was young.

SamJack's sleek silver hybrid streaked down Tollway 83 at speeds Sandra had never witnessed, let alone driven in.

"Um, Sam, I'd like to get there in one piece, you know?" she mused. SamJack cast a glance over at her.

"I am pushing the pace, but I am anything but reckless. Sooner I get you there, the calmer my brother is going to be, and that's good for all of us".

"Furthermore," he continued as he switched lanes to exit the highway, "being that we are en route to a birth, I think the fact that I am operating in service of a greater good will ensure a safe path." Finally, a smile, she thought.

"Well, I'm glad that you thought this out. Is this Oscar and Maria's first child?"

"Maria?" SamJack frowned, "It's Mirabel," he rolled the 'r' for effect.

"How you gonna catch a baby and you don't know the momma's name?"

Sandra retorted, "I am doing this as a favor to Dona Maria - she is the midwife who had been working with Mirabel." SamJack's smooth countenance had changed; his brow was furrowed as he navigated traffic towards Titi's.

Mirabel toddled over to the birth pool set up in Titi's small upstairs bedroom, disrobed, and climbed in with Oscar's help. Titi looked over to Oscar and nodded towards the pool as if to inquire if he was joining Mirabel in it. Oscar scrunched up his face and like a game show host, ran his hands down his considerable profile and smiled.

"Titi that water will spill out if I get in there." Mira grabbed Oscar's hand as a contraction took hold.

"Stay close, baby," she breathed. He knelt by the pool and rubbed her shoulders. "Love, relax and let's get my little man out into the world."

"You swear down you made a boy; I told you for the last three months it's a girl. Yes Titi?"

The doorbell chimed. While Oscar and Mirabel wrapped themselves up in the energy of the impending birth, Titi slipped out the room and headed downstairs. She shook her head and thought, all kinds of those people's laws being ignored to bring this child forth; must be some special kind of child, with some serious business to undertake here.

SamJack slipped a card into her hand as they stood at the door. "If anything goes wrong and you need a doctor, call that number on the card, and I will have someone here in 15 minutes." Sandra was incredulous.

"Not to be presumptuous, but how can you manage that

without going to the hospital?"

SamJack laughed. "Here in the city, there are lines drawn between the haves and the so-called have-nots. I have the ability to travel across said lines and in this moment, there is no room for 'have-not'."

Titi opened the door. 'Hey Ma', he pecked her on the cheek. Titi smiled and stared at Sandra.

"Are we in good hands, Sammy?"

The shark smiled. "Oh yeah, Sandra is primed and ready to usher my nephew into the world."

It was Titi's turn to snort. "Sammy, I don't know if its boy or girl, I just know that we are all here to meet a miracle." Sandra turned to SamJack.

"Thanks for getting me here in one piece, Sharky." SamJack was confused. Titi pulled Sandra in the door and grabbed SamJack's hand.

"You always do well, ahem, relatively speaking, but you really did good today, Sammy. We got it from here....you get back out there and handle your business and we'll call you as soon as he's here."

SamJack hugged Titi and shouted over his shoulder on his way to the car, "Titi, I knew you knew!"

Stella's iPad was in sleep mode as she sat trying to figure out what to put in her notes about Mirabel. At this juncture, she didn't know where Mira was, didn't know who she was with besides Oscar, and wasn't sure that she could help her. All of that piled on before she even thought about the damning words Mira directed to her at the store. The iPad suddenly came to life as Skype rang. Stella didn't recognize the name, but she answered.

The woman smiled and said, "Mira wanted me to let you know that she and the baby are safe."

The screen went blank before Stella could answer, but a wave of relief came over her.

"Finally a story that fits the file," thought Stella.

Stella opened Mira's file and voice- typed, "Client has successfully utilized resources in her community to stabilize her life, and requests release from monitoring and assistance program."

Stella had to laugh at her relief that Mira had given her closure. Meanwhile, on a quiet block across the line, in the midst of the laws and powers that shapeshift the order of life with a click of a button, there was a parallel wave of relief, as a process as old as the memories stored in stones, culminated in an arrival of a healthy, boisterous...girl.

CONTRIBUTOR BIOS

Jason Harris - Editor

Jason's work was first published by Pearl Cleage in the *Catalyst*, and his work has also appeared in *Black Enterprise* magazine and various community based print and online publications. For the past 15 years he has worked in the IT field, and he currently works in a Baltimore area high school as a support engineer. In addition to his IT experience, Jason co-founded the Baltimore chapter of the International Capoeira Angola Foundation, a cultural arts group that teaches and propagates the martial art Capoeira Angola. His work can be seen online at www.newfuturism.com. This is his first book.

Maya Harris - Copy Editor

Maya Harris is a 1996 graduate of Virginia Union University. She spent four years teaching English in Hartford Public Schools before returning to Virginia in 2001 to teach in Henrico County Public Schools. She currently teaches in Hanover County, where she is the head of an English Department for a public High School. Ms Harris serves as a coach for student slam poets and founded the African-American Studies group at her current school. Ms. Harris is a former editor for a Richmond Indie publishing company and continues to freelance for local writers, poets, and students. She is currently working on a biography of Octavia Butler.

Sierra McCleary-Harris - Layout Editor

Sierra McCleary-Harris is a Baltimore native currently working as a layout editor for a trade publication in New York City. She recently earned an M.A. from New York University's Arthur L. Carter Journalism Institute, and prior to that, graduated Magna Cum Laude from Susquehanna University in Selinsgrove, Pennsylvania, where she served as the editor of the school's student paper.

Dirk Joseph - Art

Dirk Joseph is a multi-disciplinary visual artist and art teacher. He has been employed as a "teaching artist" by organizations such as The Baltimore Office of Promotions and the Arts working in conjunction with the Board of Education to implement art residencies in Baltimore's Public schools. He recently completed a stint teaching art at the Baltimore Leadership School for Young Women. He has exhibited his art at numerous galleries, restaurants, educational and cultural institutions such as the Rush Art Gallery in Chelsea NY, the National Black Theater in Harlem NY, the BHO Gallery in Canada and throughout Baltimore. His artwork can be viewed at www.aziarts.com.

Tonika Berkley

Tonika Berkley is a writer, educator, archaeologist and healer. Her blog, Deeper Shades of Soul, serves as an online resource for parents and educators working towards the intellectual, physical, emotional and spiritual development of accelerated and multisensory-sensitive children of color. Ms. Berkley has been journal writing for 15 years and writing poetry and creative non-fiction for 5 years. Her literary influences are Octavia Butler, Philip K. Dick, Ayn Rand and Steven King. "Bravebird" is her first foray into short story writing.

Raven Ekundayo

Raven Ekundayo wears many hats as an "Artrepreneur"; he is a CEO, Actor, Poet, Editor and Host. A graduate of the Baltimore School for the Arts, for the past 6 years Raven has run his own company, Ravolution Multimedia, LLC, which produces a web based multimedia publication, eXcapethematriX.com. He has also served as the At Large Editor for *Gabriel Magazine*, which is based in Baltimore, MD. In September 2008, Raven created and began hosting a monthly event called 'Storytellers' at the Eubie Blake Center in Baltimore. In the wake of a string of highly publicized suicides by LGBT youths around the United States, in 2010 Raven launched a non-profit organization, The Love Movement, which serves as a platform for addressing prejudice and bigotry through the advocacy of peace and love. Raven currently resides in New York City, where he is pursuing an acting career and writing his first book.

Marialuz Castro Johnson - Translator

Born in Ecuador and raised in the United States, Marialuz has dedicated her career to empowering girls, women and families throughout the different stages of life. She has worked supporting women in the childbearing year, educating adolescent and adult parents, linking families to social and medical services as well as advocating for the wellness of girls, women and families.

Indirah Estelle

Indirah Estelle, a 2012 graduate of Loch Raven High School, has worked and performed for numerous non-profit organizations in the Baltimore area, including Youth Dreamers Inc, Wombwork Productions and Youth As Resources. She is currently a freshman at Baltimore City Community College. This is her first published work.

Kenisha Groomes-Faulk

Kenisha Groomes-Faulk is a writer living, learning, and loving in Washington, DC. The wife and mother of three holds a BA in Africana Studies with a minor in Political Science from SUNY Albany and is pursuing an MBA in Economic Crime and Fraud Management. Her writing reflects her commitment towards the African Diasporal experience, told against the backdrop of sociopolitical and economic factors on the world stage. She loves all things African and Brazilian, including capoeira, samba, and dance. Contact her at bithenewblack@gmail.com.

Mirlande Jean-Gilles

Mirlande Jean-Gilles is a writer and illustrator. Her fiction has won numerous awards including: The QBR-Toni Cade Bambara Award for Fiction, The Bronx Writer's Center-Van Lier Award and the Frederick Douglass Creative Arts Center Fellowship for Young African American Writers. Her writing has been published in the literary journals: *The Caribbean Writer*, *African Voices Magazine* and *New Millennium Writings*. Her poetry has been in the anthologies *The Oxford Book of Caribbean Verse*, *Beyond the Frontier* and also in *Chorus*.

Fernando Quijano III

Fernando Quijano III is the President of the Baltimore Chapter of the Maryland Writers' Association & author of *From the Bottom Up*, an op-ed column featured on theurbantwist.com. His work has been featured in *Welter, Smile Hon, You're in Baltimore, Baltimore Fishbowl and* the anthology, *Life in Me Like Grass on Fire.* An excerpt from his unpublished novel, *Killing Lilith* was included in the Apprentice House anthology *Freshly Squeezed.* He has been featured at the Baltimore Book Festival, as well as on *Essential Sundays, Last Rites, Stoop Storytelling* & *The Signal* on WYPR. In his spare time, he volunteers to lead free writing workshops. Fernando was recently awarded a 'B' grant for his writing by the William G. Baker Jr. Memorial Fund. You can find more of Fernando's work at thewordpimpspits.blogspot.com.

Alexis M. Skinner

Artist-scholar Alexis M. Skinner devotes her talents to writing and performing in the spirit of nommo, an African concept that imbues each individual with the power to create with intention. A Baltimore native, she is presently an Instructor of Theatre at the University of Arkansas at Pine Bluff where she is instilling in young artists the tools necessary to follow their passion and the discipline to achieve their dreams. She has written several plays and short stories, including a staged retelling of the classic Little Red Riding Hood. You can read her work on her blog Nommo Rising: Creating Conscious www.nommorising.wordpress.com.

Devlon E. Waddell

Publisher, author, educator and activist Devlon E. Waddell has found life in the written word. As Founder of dewdrop Collective Publishing and Co-Founder of dewMore Baltimore this native Baltimorean, husband and father of two dedicates his life to the edification of others through the intensely honest examination of his own internal dialogue. He is the author of two collections of creative nonfiction, *Them Bradsher Boys & other tall tales & short stories*, published in 2011, and *Syrup Sandwich: a life of measured progression*, published in 2009.

CPSIA information can be obtained
at www.ICGtesting.com
Printed in the USA
LVHW04s0234160618
580967LV00006B/72/P